ASPECTS
of NATURE

We gratefully acknowledge the support of the Canada Council for the Arts and the Ontario Arts Council for our publishing program. We also acknowledge the financial support of the Government of Canada through the Canada Book Fund.

Cover design: Val Fullard

Aspects of Nature is a work of fiction. All the characters and situations portrayed in this book are fictitious and any resemblance to persons living or dead is purely coincidental.

Library and Archives Canada Cataloguing in Publication

Rabinowitz Green, Rhoda, 1935-, author
     Aspects of nature : short stories / by Rhoda Rabinowitz Green.

(Inanna poetry and fiction series)
Issued in print and electronic formats.
ISBN 978-1-77133-281-1 (paperback).--ISBN 978-1-77133-282-8 (epub).--
ISBN 978-1-77133-284-2 (pdf)

     I. Title. II. Series: Inanna poetry and fiction series

PS8635.A225A86 2016   C813'.6   C2016-900304-3
                                              C2016-900305-1
Printed and bound in Canada

Inanna Publications and Education Inc.
210 Founders College, York University
4700 Keele Street, Toronto, Ontario M3J 1P3 Canada
Telephone: (416) 736-5356   Fax (416) 736-5765
Email: inanna.publications@inanna.ca Website: www.inanna.ca

MIX
Paper from
responsible sources
FSC® C004071

ASPECTS
of NATURE

stories by
Rhoda Rabinowitz Green

inanna poetry & fiction series

INANNA PUBLICATIONS AND EDUCATION INC.
TORONTO, CANADA

To my wonderful family and friends

Table of Contents

The Wind At Her Back

THE OPENING IS HERS ALONE. The silence in the small amphitheatre is that of a hundred breaths held, waiting. For an instant black and white keys blur as Miriam at the Steinway positions her hands on the keyboard, closes her eyes, calls up in her mind the tranquil opening chords of the *Archduke Trio*'s third movement, leans in to the piano and begins. Ari allows them to play uninterrupted to the end, but when they finish, he slowly and deliberately gets up from his front row seat, walks to a spot between Sasha and Izzy, and claims centre stage.

"But, of course, it is fine playing. Very professional. And you do play with much depth of feeling," he says in his studied European way, his accent marked, though not harsh like some. Well, he's learned to start with something positive, Miriam notes, but she knows what's to follow.

"This middle movement is ... is to climb Mount Everest. It is Beethoven at his most majestic. But we are not here for compliments. So. We must begin ... Yes, Miriam, the sound is right for Beethoven, full, weighty, sombre, but you, you play note by note. You must shape the phrase, it moves to here, precisely here," jabbing the exact point in the music. "Build slowly ... *pianissimo*, then more ... more ... and *move*, then open to the climax. The principle is like the stock market. Buy cheap, sell high, with a *phenomenal* sense of release ... knowing no one will ask you to do it again," his voice dropping to a hush.

1

He waits, allowing his words to resonate, then goes to his seat but turns back, still unsatisfied. "The *turn*, Miriam, the turn must speak, with you it is just a turn. And what is it you do here? It is an accent, yes, but how do you play it? Beethoven was deaf, he didn't limp!" To Izzy, his violin at the ready, "Closer to the bridge." To Sasha, "Weightier, more bow. Don't reprint the music, re-*feel* it! You must ASK…" he stretches the word, drawing his arm across an imaginary cello, "yes, *ask* the notes to be long, then, "You have a story Sasha, but it doesn't interest me."

Typical, Miriam thinks, listening to appreciative laughter from the crowd. She catches Sasha's wince, how his serious face, more youthful than his years, reflects his pain.

"Thoughts are expressed by sonorities, Sasha. What sonority do you want?" Ari persists.

"I don't know," Sasha answers after a long thoughtful pause.

"You don't know. Good. Like the weather, you never know." The words slip easily from Ari, a glint in his eye. "Play again, please, from where you come in together."

He returns to his seat, opens the score and waits, patient, intent, everyone's eyes on him. In the few moments it takes Sasha and Izzy to retune, Miriam examines Ari: high forehead, dark hair, greying, receding at the temples, sensitive mouth, strong jaw, solid build; in his fifties, some twenty-five years older than she. Escaped the deterioration of age, *willed* it so, she smiles to herself. His dress today is casual: gun-metal cardigan, white shirt open at the collar, neat trousers, loafers. Comfortable with himself.

What is it she feels for him? Awe? Admiration? For choosing to be more whole than bitter after *Bergen Belsen*, greater, not less than himself? He allows only brief glimpses, snapshots long forgotten in a dark closet, stumbled upon. Just a boy then. Vienna; his home … he's given only hints, the rest she's imagined: leather armchairs, carved sideboards, huge punch bowls, silver candlesticks, hand cut crystal; music room, grand piano ... family; a first love? All, gone. It's difficult to envision him with a mother and father, sisters, brothers. His gaze burns into her. Moments stretch like minutes. She looks over at Sasha: head bent to one side, ear almost touching the strings, listening, tuning, listening. Violin upright on one knee, Izzy waits, silently practices fingering a difficult passage. Sasha gives one last twist of a peg, one last gentle pluck of the C string, and finally satisfied, embraces his cello, a lover, looks over at Miriam, raises his bow, nods; he's ready. At the instant it touches the string she and Izzy join with him, their bodies moving to the music's demands, three instruments breathing as one. Its ripe fullness, interplay of voices, the tactile pleasure of fingertips against keys, the rightness, this is what Miriam loves, total immersion in the moment, fully lived without burden of past or future. Her concentration ends abruptly as she becomes aware of Ari beside her.

"But you drown them with this lava of noise!" Ari says, sliding onto the bench, displacing her. "You overwhelm them with feeling! Why must you always feel more than everyone else?" She stands awkwardly by as he imitates her playing in a manner so exaggerated the pounding makes her wince. "I will show you. Where the crescendo begins, from there Sasha, Izzy."

A leader but not leading, following but not a follower, Ari supports so reliably they're suddenly freed, reaching a new artistry. Even Sasha and Izzy are astonished. The audience aahs, claps. Does Ari know how he's reduced her by contrast?

"Aaach! Beethoven asks for clarity and you sound like you work in a noodle factory!" he flings at them after they try again. "He demands simplicity and you are Hungarian! He asks for shimmering, you offer flat champagne!" Still hurt, Miriam laughs, in spite of herself, along with everyone. Ari's genuinely surprised, delighted.

"This whole section..." Sasha protests, standing up to him.

The audience squirms and gasps, but Sasha persists until Ari's patience is at its end. Dropping all grandstanding, Ari becomes reflective.

"What you do is correct, but not right. When Liszt says something three times it is because he has nothing else to say. But you are playing Beethoven, not Liszt." Ari proceeds to sing the melody, his voice holding a dialogue with itself, indicating each nuance, pause, turn of phrase, while imitating the movements of a cellist. "And ... you two are always in agreement." He stops, allowing Sasha and Izzy to think he's offered some approval, then adds, "Neither of you ever raises his voice!"

"I had once a young man come to my home for dinner," Ari keeps on, speaking directly to Sasha. "'As my guest you have a choice,' I told him. 'You may have chicken, or chicken.' I offer you the same freedom," he finishes, smiling. Abruptly, as he did earlier, he turns serious.

"One strives for the Classical Ideal, for bal*ance*," accenting the final syllable, "for unity. Proportion is all. More than all else one must reach for that moment the soul speaks. That great moment that cannot be reached from the mind but must come from the deepest part of one's being. Not that we can indulge passion at the expense of unity, balance, proportion."

He pauses, confiding to an intimate, just themselves, alone in a parlour, "Bach is a giant, but he has never filled the spaces of my soul. For me, Ah! Schubert, Schumann, Chopin, Brahms.... When I am in their company I ask for that instant of inspiration, that unpredictable dimension that will cause the heart to stop, the earth stand still."

No one moves, breathes. Manipulated by a Master, Miriam thinks. Captivated against her will, for it is the poet Ari she loves.

"It is enough for today. We begin tomorrow with the Mendelssohn at nine, yes?" The audience groans. "All right," smiling, "Musicians need their morning rest. Ten o'clock." Only Ari seems not exhausted from the day's work.

"Miriam," Ari addresses her as Sasha and Izzy pack up. "Come tonight for a session, we have not long before your Massey Hall debut and my time is right now valuable. I leave for Paris and London the morning after you play. My studio at home, six-thirty, don't be late." He walks out of the hall without waiting for a reply.

"My studio tonight, Miriam," Izzy mimics, capturing Ari's tone and accent. "I don't know what you're doing, but I'm going home to play the way I want. You know what I think about our being here." Miriam doesn't stop him; he's a man of few words.

"What *are* we doing here?" Sasha asks after Izzy has left.

"Ari's the best, Sasha, you know it."

"He cuts us to pieces. We don't need him anymore, we're beyond it."

"No, we do. He's cutting, I know, but his criticism's a gift. That's how *he* sees it. Tell him you're hurt and he won't know what you're talking about, he won't even remember what he said."

"So much for sensitivity."

"Sash, he gives us his all, everything he knows and hears. Isn't that worth putting up with his..."

"Brutality? To you maybe, not to me, or Izzy. Maybe it's more than his coaching interests you, Miriam."

"What does that mean?"

"He's not just a coach, is he? Not just the master musician either. Maybe it's the *man* excites you."

"And maybe you'd like to be half the musician he is," she snaps.

"Or the man, Mims?"

Only Sasha calls her that. Once he said, "I'm steady and devoted and I love you." She was stunned, laughed, dismissing him; the look on his face told her how deeply she'd hurt him. He's never brought it up again, but his eyes reveal he still feels the same.

"He's a big ego, all consuming, and he'll bend your talent to his," Sasha says quietly. "It isn't what you've said, it's what you haven't. You've not denied anything about Ari, or how you feel," keeping his gaze fixed. She looks away and doesn't answer. Without comment, he leaves. Her silence disturbs her. It's dusk and the room is growing dark. Miriam looks out, watching for Sasha. Lights along the narrow tree lined street come on, casting their amber glow on falling snowflakes and the row of brownstones. A mounted policeman rides slowly by and through closed windows Miriam hears, faintly, the clop-clopping of hooves on cobblestones. Without turning, cello under his arm, Sasha waves as he passes and walks on. Miriam bundles up against the cold, gathers her music, and hurries out into the night.

*

She arrives at Ari's precisely at six-thirty. She wouldn't dare be late. Snow's falling heavily, lies like a fleecy comforter over the parkette in the centre of Rittenhouse Square. Squinting, she tries seeing through the hoary swirl, drifting confetti, the world a glass paperweight, beautiful, alive with motion.

Two-Twenty-Two. Large gold numbers edged in black stand out clearly. Miriam runs up the few steps to the once grand mansion and into the lobby. As she steps from the elevator, she hears Ari — Chopin, G *minor Ballade* — and enters his apartment without knocking. She sits on the supple, brown leather sofa, waiting. He doesn't look up. Chopinesque melodies fill the room, questioning, answering, now agitated, now tender; cadenzas weave a filigree, interlacing arpeggios leap upward, downward, playful dolphins, cascade forth, die away. She marvels all over again at his playing.

The room suits him, the man *and* his music, Miriam thinks: two baby grand pianos facing one another belly to belly, dark wood floors, Persian area rugs, gleaming walnut desk, book lined walls; above his head, on the wall, autographed pictures of Artur Rubinstein and Eugene Ormandy embracing him in one, a smiling Jack Benny with his violin in another ... *To my dear friend, Ari.* A fire in the fireplace spreads its warm glow, flickers its light across her face.

Her thoughts fall away with the dying sounds of the *Ballade.* Ari moves away from the keyboard and they exchange a few words; he's not one for casual talk. They'll work the whole of the evening, longer if necessary, first on her program for New York's Ninety-Second Street Y.

"There are a million ways to play that passage Miriam, but I don't like your way," she hears Ari. She's been working on the Brahms for months, yet he remains dissatisfied. He sings the *Intermezzo,* its wistful melody, tender assertion; its comment, deeper, throatier. Miriam's fingers pick up where his voice leaves off. Then, Schumann, *Kinderszenen, the Kind im Einschlummern.* She's played this before but it's become stale, lost its poetry. Ari word paints: sleeping baby, pink and angelic, dreaming; quick movements under closed lids, lashes flicker, tiny plump fingers twitch ... a sigh, a shake, pouty baby lips tease a smile, about the dream? Ari cradles his arms and sways, listen to the rocking it says. It flows, Ari to Miriam, and from her fingers.

Debussy doesn't come so easily; *Estampes,* Gardens in the Rain, languorous Spanish rhythms, gauzy sounds, gossamer, chiffon and lace, feathers and thistledown. Where's the spine? No, the Impressionists elude her. Ari says nothing. Then, his words, slow and measured: "It is not life or death, Miriam; it is only one phrase. Get the most from it. What you cannot get today, you will get tomorrow. If you get it all now, what's to live for?"

Finally they move on to the Concerto. Winner of the Philadelphia Young Artists' Competition, she'll debut with Beethoven's *Fourth* under Muti at the Academy of Music. Ari's never been more demanding. They work, Ari at the second piano, playing the orchestral score, moulding, weaving parts, an elaborate tapestry. Value each note, increase here, decrease there, half-pedal this place, none there. In the process she loses the emotion and the fingers do strange things. "Ari this passage is…" She stops herself; no protesting. How can it be, a novice again! Hours of painstaking exploration, depressing keys slowly, quickly, from the key, above the key, peaceful wrist or active; technique in the tradition of Czerny, Cramer, Kullak, of Liszt and Rubinstein; legato, legacy of Field and Chopin; pedal, touch, colour, of Debussy and Ravel, Gieseking and Casadesus, all handed down to Miriam through Ari Zachar, everything she's ever learned marshalled to achieve the ideal he hears in his mind. He's a conduit, faith healer, laying on hands. From others he demands the soul's breath.

Getting up from the second piano, Ari stands near Miriam, instructing, "Measure your energy from the first phrase to the last. Play again the beginning." She does as he says, playing the tranquil opening chords once more. "Too much, too much … hold back, you must save the emotion," Ari directs. "Now go to the *dev*elopment. Give more but not everything, save it for the climax." He takes her from instant to instant to the finale. "Hold nothing back now, give us your strength, your heart. We have waited for this moment."

At last Ari's satisfied. "Yes, you will be ready," he says. Walking over to the window, he gazes out onto the square. Miriam follows, and standing beside him, looks out at the still falling snow. The parkette lies beneath a glistening white shroud, elms stretch frothy arms and snow warmed benches cast long, slat shadows onto virgin whiteness.

"I leave for London this week, Miriam."

"How long will you be gone?"

"One month, six weeks.… It is a long tour. Paris, Avignon, Brussels, London, Amsterdam, Vienna … Israel."

"It is grueling," she says, pondering. What drives this man who allows the world to see into his soul, reveals more than most dare consider yet remains so apart? Searching his face, she asks, finally, "Ari, can I make it?" He shrugs.

"Do I have a crystal ball? Such questions I cannot answer. You must hunger for it."

"As you do?"

"The more I play, the more I need to play. I can never get enough; it is what nourishes me." They become silent, watching the hushed undisturbed world below. At last he turns to her, a direct, unwavering look. "One searches for a perfection that can never be reached, for inspiration. It is not enough to sail when the wind is at your back. You must learn to sail when the wind is in your face."

"But is it enough for you, Ari?"

"Enough? It is my life." She catches a flicker of yearning in eyes normally so concentrated with purpose. "It is a lonely business, it is not for everyone. I have been not so fortunate to have more. Some things are predestined not to be." He looks back out the window, then as if to himself, almost a whisper, "There is room for only one talent and all must bend to it." Sasha's words echo.

"We are asked to make choices," he finishes simply.

For a moment they are still, alone with their thoughts.

"I have never known a talent not wanting to be better than the master. Is this not true, Miriam?" directly to her. "Is this not so?" he repeats, then moving away, walks over to stoke the fire.

She goes to him, hears herself murmur, *Ari?* but in her mind, his name on her lips. In the quiet, flickering light dances across their faces. Extending her arm, she *feels* the imagined roughness of his sweater under her fingers, his arm straining to her touch ... and pulls back. She senses his desire to reach out, not daring, like herself; afraid to breathe, afraid of the moment, its fragility, shatterable as fine glass.

"Come, you will be ready," he says firmly. "I have now work of my own."

She sees in the set of his jaw, his eyes, the almost imperceptible shift of his body, that he's retreated behind his first, his *only* love. He wouldn't allow it to be otherwise.

*

At the Steinway, statuesque in a simple black velvet gown, Miriam peers out through the glare of stage lights into the darkened hall. She makes out Izzy and Sasha, scans the rows for Ari, her heart pounding. Yes, he is there, on the aisle.

The Academy is filled, the audience in plush red velvet seats, waiting; the hum of voices, silenced, programs quieted, the massive chandelier dims, withdrawing its light; Renaissance wall paintings recede in shadow. The stage door opens, Muti appears, strides quickly to the podium, applause crescendos and fades, the hall dark, hushed, orchestra ready. She's been preparing physically and mentally for this hour. He turns to Miriam. The opening is hers alone.

Hold back, hold back, save the emotion. She begins, plays the wondrous opening G major chords not only with her hands but with her soul. In the instant, at the same time out of it, listening, evaluating, instantaneously adjusting, she performs as never before. Passages demanding strength are of little consequence, executed without strain, the energy disguised. Lyric moments sing, each tone flows from one to the next, liquid gold, yet hangs in midair, round, distinct, separate but strung together, pearls on a string. *Give more, not everything, save for the climax.* Ari taught her well. *Hold nothing back now, your strength, your heart ... we have waited for this moment.* Final chords linger, float suspended, disappear, existing only as memory.

No one moves. Timeless seconds ... burst of applause. Quickly she steps to the front of the stage, bows, smiles, reaches out to the crowd. Her eyes move immediately to Ari.

His seat is empty.

It is a lonely business ... grueling; practice, travel, the anxiety of performance ... but then the supreme exhilarating joy of success! *I've never known a talent not wanting to be better than the Master. Is that not right, Miriam?* Soon it will be morning and Ari will be in Paris. She closes her eyes and imagines him walking along the banks of the Seine and through the Tuilleries, a light snow falling. His eyes will drink in Sisleys, Renoirs and Pissarros at the Jeu de Paume; he'll stroll Paris streets and sip wine in the cafés of Montmartre, lunch on baguettes and cheese; breathe in the smells of *les charcuteries et boulangeries*, soak up sounds of buskers, their Frenchy voices, their accordions. He'll play Chopin's *F Minor*. Paris will be beautiful ... even in winter.

Author's note: The pianist and master teacher, Ari, in "The Wind At Her Back," is a fictionalized character, a composite of my two most influential professors of piano, Maryan Filar (See Finding Maryan in this collection) and Menahem Pressler, of The Beaux Arts Trio; a rendering of remembered instruction and interactions — conversations — held over many years; and a great deal from my imagination. Nevertheless, I want to acknowledge Nicholas Delbanco and his portrait of The Beaux Arts Trio, in his book of the same name. It was an invaluable source for my research on the world of concert chamber music and in drawing the character of Ari.

You Make Your Decision

*T*O THE WOMAN (GOD) SAID ... *(Because thou hast eaten of the tree of which I commanded thee not to eat) I will greatly increase thy travail and thy pregnancy; with pain thou shalt bear children; and to thy husband shall be thy desire, and he shall rule over thee.*

...And to Adam he said, because thou hast hearkened to the voice of thy wife ... curst be the ground on thy account; with toil shalt thou eat (of) it all the days of thy life ... In the sweat of thy face shalt thou eat bread, until thou return to the ground....

*

Once upon a time, there was a farmer and his wife. Everyday they argued over the same thing, the division of their labour. The farmer didn't understand what his wife did with her day; she didn't know how to carry out his. She complained of the children, chores ... baking, washing, ironing, cleaning. And so the husband provided his wife with the best of modern conveniences: washer, dryer, dishwasher, Hoover. But in spite of all he'd provided, she wasn't satisfied; the old complaints were simply replaced with a new problem: leisure time. The farmer tried to teach his wife to mend fences, milk the cows, bring in the harvest, but she was impossible. And so she turned to foolishness: quilting bees, bake-offs, visiting other farmer's wives who had the same problem: leisure time.

And there another tale begins....

*

Laughing her head off, the secretary ushered the young woman into the Dean's broadloomed office. (Not *really* laughing her head off; it only seemed that way.)

Laughing his head off, the Dean gestured to a chair in front of his massive oak desk. "Have a seat, have a seat," he said.

What have I done to deserve your laughter? the girl asked with her eyes. She didn't understand then, nor did she in the years that followed. (I remember the humiliating self-doubt.) But why *laughter?* A steel-booted kick, a private joke, with herself the victim. Think how she must have felt that sunny southern-Indiana afternoon in August 1956, far from home (Toronto), seated in his sound-choked office, surrounded by walls of weighty music texts and bound scores, the *butt of derision.*

He hadn't answered her unspoken question, not immediately, only smiled back, a stupid pasted grin (that's how it appeared); didn't answer until she brought up the letter. Three-paged, typed, single-spaced. Remember? she jogged his memory.

That jogged his laughter. Why should he grant her money? He'd found it amusing that she'd spill out she *wants, needs, (dies) to do thus and so,* would utter such melodramatic desires, beginning naively with one's name, introducing oneself. Who starts a letter that way?

She hadn't intended to be amusing. These outpourings expressed childhood fantasies, youthful ambitions. Everyone wants to be a great something, The Man commented. But she'd *written* "fine;" *fine* pianist; fine was not great.

It all began long ago, she explained (intensely serious), in her grandfather's Cabbagetown home where she listened to her mother, a raven-haired beauty, playing on their old Heinzman piano. *Listen to the Mocking Bird ... listen to the mocking bird, oh the mocking bird is singing all the day ...* singing with quivery voice, a warbler, and joy tinged with the melancholy of generations of Hasidic cantors and mournful fiddlers from the *shtetl.*

He found this amusing too. What had all this to do with the present? he seemed to be asking, his fingers forming a tent at his (smiling) lips.

She tried another tack.

One evening, no longer a child, but a young woman of sixteen, she'd climbed, breathless, to the uppermost heights of Massey Hall to hear the great Gieseking. *Schumann, Arabesque* ... a sound, simple, hushed, serene, floated upward, reached with, oh, such effortless clarity and resonance her insides trembled, the bridge of her nose tingled. *Debussy, Chopin.*... At the Bechstein, he brushed the keys with fine, elongated fingers (spanning an octave), causing a spontaneous unteachable thing to happen not simply *to* the notes, but *between*, something rhythmic and sonoric, moving forward and holding back, cheating and robbing, giving and adding; something called beauty and genius. All, liquid, each tone, phrase, shift in sentiment, flowed one from the other without jarring or angularity, the keyboard an orchestra. When he'd finished, gauzy tone-clusters lingered, cocooned in a profound silence no one was willing to break, dying their own death. She knew then what path she must take.

That is how she expressed herself.

But the Dean had his own story: *The tale of the farmer and his wife.*... "You understand?" he asked.

His unlined face and faded blue eyes made his gaze appear genuine, the question innocent. She turned quickly from him. For a moment, until she could regain her composure, she concentrated on the treed grounds outside, the great limestone buildings, students everywhere. When she turned back, her glance fixed on the sheen of his expensive suit.

"You understand?" he repeated. "*I'll bet on the men, who make careers; women make bambinos.*"

There followed a chasm of silence (I remember to this day) through which she fell, plunging downward through light-years.

He smiled (once more) and glanced at his watch, then stood, taking up all the space. "Come now, my dear," extending his huge hand, "You made your decision the moment you said I DO."

On her way down the long corridor, she imagined him singing a song about a mocking bird, and laughing his head off.

*

You play very well, my dear, but what have you been doing all these years?

*

She's crying her head off. Not really, it just feels that way to Jenny.

Standing in their family room (anywhere down South) amongst empty, open boxes (boxes, boxes....)

"Must we go?"

"We're going, Jen." (Kindly.) "Can't be helped."

"Three years, we're never more than that anywhere."

"Jenny, if I want the promotion, we move."

"But to *Alberta*?"

"To Alberta. The Company says that's where I'm needed, it's as simple as that."

"But my trio.... We're just now sounding like an ensemble."

Gently admonishing, "Jenny...."

"The conservatory ... the wisteria, all purple and tumbling over the portico ..."

"I can't afford to turn it down, Jen."

"Our house ... the iris ... pink and purple and yellow ..."

"Our *family* needs it, Jenny."

"For your career."

"For my career."

"What about mine?"

"It's portable, isn't it? You can teach anywhere, play anywhere?"

"But I keep starting over, spinning wheels. And with the children…"

"Jen, we don't go, I don't go anywhere in the Company. Everything we've worked for levels out. It's for us, for the kids, down the road."

"But can't you tell the Company…?"

"You don't *tell* the Company anything."

(Long pause. Subdued.) "We go round and round about it, Jenny. Every time you say okay, you'll try, it reverts back the next day. There doesn't seem any way out of it and we can't keep this up, so … I guess we stay; I'll work it out."

"Well I don't want to be responsible for taking you out of the line of succession. It's too heavy."

"Then what do you want, Jen?"

"I guess I wanted it to come from you, at the beginning."

"That's expecting too much. I can't tell what's in your head. Look Jen, you can't have it all ways. I said we won't go, doesn't mean I have to be happy about it. You *can* play anywhere."

"We'll go."

She is crying her eyes out. Really.

*

Surrounded by dark green walls and floors, wine-purple venetian blinds, Jenny sits at the dining-room table in their rented Hampstead terrace house. Not *really* almost-black walls and blinds; it just feels that way. By British standards it's a good home, solid middle class. Under the cold light from the overhead, her head in her hands, Jenny cries her heart out.

Her friends say how lucky she is, a year in London, on the Company. After so many years you get a sabbatical; it's a new policy. Ira said to rent a Steinway, not this Broadwood upright, this toy. So what if a baby grand would take up the whole of the living room, so what if it costs a lot, they can afford it. Why does she worry about things like that?

She's working on a Bach Prelude and Fugue, a good way to

get her fingers moving again. Exaggerating, lifting each finger high, she follows the Theme through the three voices and repeats the last eight bars over; and again and again. Bach has never gratified the cravings of her heart, not totally, but it's the fingers she's interested in just now.

Her mind is elsewhere, all over the place. Didn't used to be that way. Used to be she could concentrate for hours on end. The technique comes back easily; the talent somehow matures even when it's not in use; the focus slips away.

It's raining, the usual warm drizzle. Ira is out looking at Saabs and Audis and Karmen Gias; Jenny wanted him to buy a used London taxi, big and black and no-nonsense, but he wanted something sexier. She ought to be out *doing* something too, after all she's in London for the year, and here she sits repeating the same bars, the same Theme turning this way and that, to what end? That question would never have entered her mind at one time.

Perhaps she ought to go poke around in Harrods, or have tea in Fortnum and Masons, or spend a few hours at the Tate.

This cut-off feeling, adrift with no land in sight, no markers, won't leave. Oh, some of it is wondrous — the chaos of roses all yellow and pink and velvety red in the front garden, the vegetable patch in the back, even the Alice-in-Wonderland rabbit she and Ira had promised to care for, always digging out from under the picket fence, running away; if they were lucky, Ira said, cursing, the damn thing would get lost or run over.

So much disorienting newness, and she hasn't even the excuse of speaking Hindi or Farsi, or Arabic. She takes too long in the queue at the butcher's deciding between cuts of meat; sawdust ... bloodied aprons ... hanging carcasses ... at Loblaws she would've grabbed some pre-packaged fillets. At the greengrocer's she forgets to bring her own brown bag; in a cab she panics predicting the fare —how much is two pound ten pence *really*? In and out twisty streets, their names falling away from one block to the next. Is she being *had*? Will she ever dare drive the circuses? Even the ring of the telephone is strange — two short rings at once, a high-up *brring-brring*, loud and assertive. And no friend's voice at the other end. No one who's been on leave ever tells you all this. Oh, so much, her head feels all foggy, like a constant allergy. Ira seems to find none of it upsetting. He's busy going to the theatres and museums and looking for a car.

She'll go to the knit shop, take her "brolly" and walk. Not certain why it's so comforting, she's taken up knitting. Perhaps there's some security in even stitches and row upon row of predictable sameness. But she keeps dropping a stitch and having to rip out and start over. Maybe she'll finish this sweater for Ira before the year is out. Maybe she won't.

Ira pulls up in front in the green Lada their landlord left for them. Ira says it drives like an eighteen-wheeler (true); it needs a three-point turn no matter how wide the street and the two of them together pulling on the steering wheel. He curses the rabbit and the Lada equally.

Jenny watches Ira walk through roses grown wild and up to his shoulders; his long, tough-lean frame (his hair incorrigible as the garden growth) disappears through the gate leading around to the back. Seconds later she hears the back kitchen door slam.

"Goddamn rabbit's dug out under his pen for the tenth time!" Ira shouts. "Shit! Now I've got to hunt up and down the street again for it. Got the whole neighbourhood looking for that rotten rabbit."

"Oh, come on Ira! Rabbit's not that bad. It gets us to meet people, like children do. Wait until Steve gets home, he'll look for it."

"Real estate agent call?"

He's been asking everyday if there's been a call from their Toronto agent. She shakes her head, no, doesn't look at him. Thoughts run through her head: eight years in *one* house ...

funny, how attached ... half the boys' lives, all their adolescent years, growing up ... our lives. Jenny sees Ira watching; his black-framed glasses make him look severe.

"I thought it was decided, Jen. You'll love Ottawa!"

Why not move? ... fine promotion (for Ira) ... kids grown, going off ... house too big without them ... Toronto expensive ... traffic congested ... new Condo market hot.... Now's the time....

"I found us a great place. You *liked* the plans!"

(Had she?) "I did promise to try it."

"I don't know what more I can say, Jen. Come on, it'll be terrific. I know it's not Toronto or Lawrence Park, but listen, it's a chance to choose exactly what you want — Jacuzzi, bidet, whatever. And..." Ira goes over to Jenny and takes her by the shoulders, "it gives us a whole new freedom. Just you and me again, like we were." Ira can be romantic.

"But what about the kids? If they have to come back to live in the house again? That's happening these days, you know. Besides, Toronto's their home. And what if Marty doesn't 'find himself' this year?"

"Either he'll be in school or out working and in his own place."

"It's too soon ... I mean, we still have years of, well, kids and their friends, and..."

"Do we? Or is it wishful thinking? You're not going to buy a house as big as the one we own now, are you?" incredulous.

"But the new place isn't designed for a family, Ira. Oh! I don't know why we're arguing about the condo. It's moving to Ottawa that's..."

"And I've got a chance to move up to the number two spot in the Company, and the top spot in Ottawa. That offer won't come again." Ira's voice has turned sharp, then convincing. "It's a chance for you too, Jenny; you can really commit yourself to your music, like when you started. What's to stop you now?"

"Start again? In a strange place?"

"There are plenty of musicians in Ottawa, Jenny."

"Businessmen and bureaucrats. That will be our circle. Besides, Ira, you're missing the point…"

"Look, if you don't want to do it, speak up now." Ira looks exasperated. "We have to stop going around and around. I already told you how important it is to me. If we stay in Toronto, after all we've worked for …" He shrugs with his hands and lets them fall heavily to his sides, a gesture of futility. "Well, you'd better decide soon because the Company expects me to take over in Ottawa by the end of the year … July … August the *latest*, soon as we get back from London. And I'm expecting the real estate agent to call with an offer any time now. *They* think we're selling our house, you know."

Jenny nods; it says I know, I know. This is what happens after their discussions, more like persuasions; she sees the logic of the situation and calms down, but her insides begin to churn just *thinking* about giving up the Lawrence Park house. Why is it she finds it so impossible to say yes unconditionally, or no, I don't want to?

Once she managed to say, "Ira, don't we have sense enough to know when we've found a place we're happy and stop looking elsewhere? We've got a good life right here in Toronto," and Ira'd said, "Fine, if that's what you want, we'll forget it," then taking the copy from his desk, with expansive gestures tore up the condo Offer-To-Buy. "I'll call the Ottawa agent straight-away and tell her not to turn it in," and with that he (dramatically) threw the torn pieces, confetti, into the air. Jenny's heart fell along with the paper bits. "That's it, done!" he finished.

"Ira!"

"Well, you don't expect me to do what you want and still be happy about it, do you? Must I agree with you when I don't?"

"I'll try it," she consented.

Ira goes out to look for the rabbit. Jenny watches him walk down the block. Next door, the two elderly Misses Johnson help their older sister from the Wheel Transport van and up the walk. That's another strangeness, Jenny thinks. All the old people on the block. Miss Johnson, eighty-eight, taking care of Miss Johnson, ninety-three, looking after Miss Johnson just turned one hundred. Yesterday, Jenny saw a limousine pull up, delivering birthday congratulations from the Queen. Back home in Toronto, the Miss Johnsons are kept out of sight; to have it otherwise is as rare as shopping at the butcher instead of Loblaws for the plastic-wrapped stuff.

Jenny picks up her knitting and goes into the living room. She'll knit-one, pearl-two for a while and wait for Steve to come home and Ira to return with the rabbit. And for the phone to ring.

When the phone does ring, it isn't their agent. It's their eldest son Marty calling (collect). He'd decided not to join them in London this year. They'd given him the choice, but Ira said not to dissuade him, it was best he sort his life out on his own (away from his father; there's the rub). Jenny thought it best they *all* stay home.

"Let him grow up," Ira said.

"Give him space," Dr. Miller advised.

"You're not going to leave him alone, are you?" Jenny's mother exclaimed.

Steve asked in a pout, "Why's he always spoiling everything? And how come you and Dad are always talking about *Marty?*"

"Your brother needs our support right now. He's having a tough time finding himself," Jenny answered (she's always explaining one to the other).

Every word over the phone with Marty tugs at Jenny. As if a TV camera were transmitting a transatlantic picture, Jenny sees his sad eyes, large and dark like Ira's. Last evening, she dreamed he came to visit and didn't say a word the whole time, just made the bed he slept in, kept tucking in the covers and smoothing them down. When he was about to leave for Toronto, she grabbed him by the shoulders and shook and shook him, all the while shouting, "Get your act together! Make up your mind what you want to do and *do* it," and, "What's the *problem*?" But he just looked at her with those sorrowful lost eyes, his long, sensitive face pained, black curly hair all loose and falling about like a sheep dog, and drew away.

She hears his voice through the receiver; it's breaking up, something about quitting his job, and loneliness (killing him) and how much he misses everyone (even Steve). "Steve's so pushy," is Marty's ongoing complaint.

"That's what younger brothers do to get their family's attention. He's only showing his love," is Jenny's answer. "Did you send the application to McGill yet?" she shouts through the phone, but she can't make out Marty's answer. Before hanging up, Jenny tells him please write, the phone bills are enormous, then worries she shouldn't have discouraged him from calling.

Steve and Ira come in together, no rabbit.

"Good," Ira says, "Maybe it's lost forever. Real estate agent call?"

"No, just Marty."

"How is he? Did he send in his application yet? There is a deadline, you know. He'll wait until it's too late, and then…" Ira says without waiting for her answer.

"Don't jump to conclusions, Ira. Marty knows about the deadline, he just needs time to work things out." (She's always explaining him to Ira.)

She doesn't tell Ira anything about the quitting part or the dying from loneliness part. It will just start up everything again and she'll say she knew they oughtn't to have abandoned him and he'll point out Marty had himself decided to stay behind, and what about Dr. Miller? And wasn't it the same as if the kids went off on their own?

"Steve?" Jenny asks abruptly. She's just caught a glimpse of him as he walks away and starts upstairs. "Steve … what's wrong with your eye?"

"What's wrong with his eye?" Ira asks, turning to look at him.

"Ira! How can you miss a black eye? Steve, turn around!" Yes, how could he miss it, a purply greenish black ringer around incredibly light blue eyes, strawberry-blonde curls framing the shiner, underscoring its incongruity? "And scratches all over your cheek!"

"It's an Irish Pub, Mom. There was a helluva fight with this punker, drunker'n hell. Man, did he put up a fight! They offered me a job. Not just servin' up beers. Bouncer! Man!" Steve turns and takes the stairs two at a time.

At eleven-thirty that evening the call comes; the high-up *brring-brring* echoes down the long, narrow hallway and into the living room. She and Ira both hate this room, its one redeeming feature being the French doors opening directly out to the back garden. Not one comfortable chair, not one decent light. When the phone rings, Jenny's mind is still back at the South Bank, the London Philharmonic, Orff, *Carmina Burana*, its haunting power. She pearls-two, knits-one, remembering the lights of small boats along the Thames, the brisk air as she walked over the bridge, the outline of Parliament and Big Ben. Mid-stitch, Jenny stops and looks sharply over at Ira. He's engrossed in the telly. The BBC is doing their usual in-depth news analysis — the Social Democrats have just split from Labour.

"I'll get it," Ira says, getting up quickly. Jenny follows him to the phone. "It's our agent," he mouths.

She looks at him, questioning with her eyes, but he holds up his hand as if to say "Hold on," and keeps nodding his head, "Uh-huh, Uh-huh..." Finally, "Right. Just a minute." His eyes are bright and he's smiling, a big excited smile, his hand over the mouthpiece. "They got a buyer! Looks good, Jen. A doctor. He's got the money, solid bank account, no problem, closing date's perfect. Our price, no haggling. What do you say?"

"I didn't really expect an offer so soon..."

"Quick Jen. Make up your *mind*, she's waiting! I thought we decided. What am I to tell her, is it yes or no?"

"I ... I guess. Everything's been put in motion..."

"It's a GO!" she hears Ira exclaim into the receiver. "Congratulations, honey," he says after he hangs up. "Now all we have to do is wire confirmation."

Somewhere she remembers learning about a law of physical properties in motion. That's what she is, some kind of flying object that continues in its trajectory, picking up speed, unable to stop itself.

That evening, Jenny falls into a fitful sleep. It must be near morning when she dreams because she can remember it vividly upon waking. It's Christmas time and she's on the top floor of a high rise. In jeans and an old sweatshirt, no make-up, her auburn hair in need of cutting, Jenny looks a mess. She doesn't care. In fact, she's pleased, likes the unadorned frankness of her eyes (green, with gold flecks), the unhidden tiny freckles across her cheeks and nose. Through a wall of floor-to-ceiling windows, Jenny looks out on a fairy-tale of trees and buildings outlined with tiny white lights, and nearby on a lawn of glittering snow, a furry Spruce twinkles red, blue and tinsel. The apartment is bare except for a small menorah, all eight candles aflame, placed in a corner on the dark-stained floor, and an elaborately set dining table. Ira is there, but he seems to be visiting her and the boys who are quite young. In the midst of serving the turkey, Ira says something about saving enough to bring back to Margaret (Ira's live-in girlfriend, Jenny supposes). Suddenly the scene changes and they're all in the kitchen of their Lawrence Park home, but all else picks up as before. Jenny's carving hand freezes and the next thing she knows she's screaming "Let Margaret worry about her own fucking turkey." (This is out of character for Jenny but she likes it.) "Technically, it's my turkey," Ira is saying, "It's a gift from the Company." Now Jenny, standing in their doorway, heaves the turkey-turned-rabbit at Ira running through the rose garden toward the parked Lada. "Take your fucking rabbit, Ira. Take it!" Jenny is shouting. Across the way, the eldest Miss Johnson peers out from behind lace curtains, and the two younger Miss Johnsons step outside to see what's going on. "Oh, Merry Christmas, Misses Johnson, Merry Christmas," Jenny says sweetly, smiling broadly. "Ta, Jenny," the eldest Miss Johnson calls. Jenny turns back to screaming at Ira and the disappearing Lada, slams the door and with the bang, wakes up.

*

Jenny hears Steve storm out the front door. He and Ira have just had an argument over the earring Steve is wearing in his left ear. That's very important, which ear, Steve tried to explain, because the right is a signal you're gay. He bounded down the stairs, into the kitchen, the shiner still a proud purply green, and turned his profile to Ira.

"Do you like it, Dad?" Steve asked (naively).

"I HATE it!" Ira answered without hesitation.

"I thought you'd like it." (How could he think that?)

"Well, now you know."

"But don't you want to be more liberal?"

"NO!"

That door closed with the slam of the front door behind Steve.

"What's the matter with that kid?" Ira calls in to Jenny. (She begins to explain him to Ira, but gives it up.)

Surrounded by dark green, almost-black walls (not *really*), Jenny sits at the dining table, her head in her hands, and without warning tears well up. Why is she crying? Fights between father and son are not unusual, especially at Steve's age. What does she expect? This is the age of rebellion, spiky hair (aubergine and orange), earrings for boys, open sex. But suddenly she's weeping, and Ira is standing beside her, incredulous.

"My God, *what have I done*?" Jenny asks aloud. "What *have* I done?"

What?" Ira asks, "What have you done?" He looks helpless.

She's weeping uncontrollably now, the sobs coming in great heaves. It seems her insides will erupt. "Oh, God..." Her face is buried in her arms folded one upon the other, a nest, on the table, out of Ira's sight. He places a hand kindly on her shoulder, then withdraws it, looking truly puzzled.

*

Jenny looks out the window of the Wardair 747, but she sees nothing, no landscape, only a cotton of cloud. She's flying home to Toronto, to Marty who's in a bad way. The year's almost over; he hasn't a job or plans; he's vague about his McGill application, meaning he hasn't sent it. "Dad'll be pissed," Marty had said. "Upset," Jenny corrected, "He thinks its some kind of rebellion against him. And he's worried you're hurting yourself." (She's always explaining Ira to Marty.) Both Steve and Ira said to let him work it out, but Jenny knew what she had to do when she asked over the phone, "Do you need help, Marty?" and he answered quietly, "Yes."

Steve has stayed behind with his father to pack up; they'd reached a silent, grudging accommodation on the earring.

"What's his problem?" Steve asked.

"Give him time. A son with an earring takes a while to get used to," Jenny told Steve (explaining Ira). But Ira surprised them just before she left for Toronto — a gesture to Steve: one gold earring.

Steve has decided if he can't remain in Britain he won't go away to university, he and his brother have been *schlepped* around enough; neither have any desire to explore. All of which means they'll be at home next year. (Where's that?)

Most people on the plane are watching the movie, but Jenny has closed her eyes, listening on the headsets to the first movement of one of Bach's Brandenburg Concerti (No. 2, F minor), its piercing Baroque trumpets, hooty recorders and moving strings. She'd thought to work on Ira's sweater; it's stuffed into a plastic bag under the seat, three-quarters finished; doesn't make sense not to get it done, but she's lost interest. Maybe she'll finish, maybe she won't.

Behind closed lids, Jenny sees herself standing in the midst of boxes stacked one upon the other in a room of the Lawrence Park house. One stack is labelled with heavy black magic-marker, TO OTTAWA, another, TO LONDON, another, TO GOODWILL; a fourth, in red, reads STEVE, and the last, MARTY. She'd organized all that before they'd left for England.

The stewardess is tapping her arm, asking if she wants more coffee. "No," Jenny indicates, annoyed at the interruption. Tchaikovsky's Fifth is coming through the headsets, but Jenny doesn't remember hearing the rest of the Brandenburg. When she re-settles and closes her eyes again, she's in the centre of an empty room, the living-dining area of their new condo. It's smaller than she expected from reading plans, and the walls she and Ira thought would be so dramatic look simply crazy; not one ninety-degree angle in the place. How on earth was she to place furniture? The fireplace is at an odd angle and too near the entrance hallway; and she'd have to take a circuitous route to get from kitchen to dining area. Looking out at the city, her chest tightens; trapped, boxed in. *What if there's a fire?* Down the hall, Jenny checks out the bedrooms. Where will Steve and Marty stay? Their future wives and children, where will *they* stay? What could she and Ira have been thinking? Oh, she's screwed up everything. Royally.

Tchaikovsky blasting through the earphones, Jenny's eyes fly open, her heart skips a beat.

"What's that, dear?" an unbelievably old woman next to Jenny is asking. Jenny takes off her headphones, blinks at the woman, twice; it can't be! *Miss Johnson?*

The 747 begins its descent. As they come out of cloud, the Toronto landscape opens up — muted pre-spring brown patches shot through with veins of tired white, the last of winter. Jenny leans back against the headrest, her heart still racing, and thinks of Ira.

The way he tells her she has great legs ... that he loves when she smiles and her eyes light up. And the *talk*. What is it they talk about so much? Rain, sun on the Heath, daffodils in Hyde Park, swans on the Serpentine; movies, baseball; Turner at the Tate, his turbulent seas and splendid skies; Arrau playing Beethoven; Olivier, Richard III ... *her* music, his career; punkers, pubs; Rabbit; Quebec, will it separate; her mother, his mother; Marty, Steve.... She smiles, remembering the earring, Ira's awkward gesture.

Without him?

To lie in the dark, so vulnerably *horizontal*, a solitary figure, solitary bed, solitary room in a house of empty rooms ... the hollow space, its weight ... hurts. The only sounds are imagined: a distant trolley, its clanging bell; a far-off siren; the tread of a foot on the stairs. Seen from a mountain view, a long sleek train winding its way deep inside a canyon of dark evergreens and silence; if there's a train whistle, she wouldn't hear it.

Jenny sits forward, peers out the window at the lake below, the long stretch of harbour, Expressway, railway yards; TD Centre ... campus ... Queen's Park ... searching for her first glimpse of the airport.

Her whole being is wired, a switchboard of criss-crossed emotions. Trepidation, for one. Elation for another, on the edge of *becoming*, not unlike that high anticipation charging mind and body just before a performance.

The risk ... I'll take it. Whatever Ira's answer the Steinway will be there, always ... Chopin, Schumann, Brahms, filling the spaces of her soul.

"What's that again, dear? You don't hear so good when you get older," the frail old lady says.

"Not when you're younger, either," Jenny smiles.

She braces herself for contact with the runway. *I'll call Ira the moment my feet are (firmly) on the ground.*

Finding Maryan

IT WAS 1952. I WAS IN UNIVERSITY then, but that was not where I wanted to be. I longed with the urgency of youth and talent to be the pianist I knew I could become. I heard of Filar by way of the buzz generated by his arrival in Philadelphia. Musicians, music faculty, students around the city, all were talking about this graduate of the Warsaw Conservatory, home to Frederic Chopin. Graduate of Buchenwald and Majdanek.

He had only recently arrived in the United States, coming from a DP camp in the American Zone in Frankfurt. We heard that after the war ended he searched out famed pianist, Walter Gieseking, living in Weisbaden, and for the next five years became his protégé. He was bringing with him, then, the finest pianistic traditions of the Conservatory *and* of Gieseking. But that is a story for later. Fortunately for me, he was to be the new Piano Department Head at the Settlement School of Music. Some of the best musicians from Ormandy's Philadelphia Orchestra taught there. That Settlement was not comparable to Curtis (its Piano Head, the famed Rudolf Serkin) or New York's Julliard, was just one of the many cultural disconnects Filar faced upon his arrival. That he'd not only survived, but survived to perform with the finest orchestras, best conductors, and concert halls across Europe, made him a kind of hero, a man of significance. An aura of mystery, romance — and awe — were attached to him. I was determined to study with such an artist.

Women of those times didn't entertain notions of becoming a doctor, a lawyer or engineer, and certainly not a performing musician. Any preparation for a concert career would be done during stolen hours between classes or at night before starting on assignments. Young women like myself needed the assurance of a living, a job (it wasn't considered a career), one allowing for a family. But the urgent need to create — to communicate directly through and to the senses, feelings for which words were inadequate, drove me. Only music could convey those deepest, most nuanced feelings by way of its all-encompassing abstraction.

I made an appointment for an audition.

"What will you play?" Filar asked.

"The Eb Major Impromptu ... Shubert," I offered.

I sat down at one of two side by side grand pianos in his studio and he seated himself at the second, watching me intently. His expression was pleasant, non-threatening; still, his dress — dark suit, shirt and tie — and manner were somewhat formal, though not coldly distant.

Financial constraints had kept me from studying for over a year and I feared that by now I'd slipped into some bad playing habits. But I loved this Impromptu. Light and breezy, lyrical despite its running passages, my fingers flew easily over the keys. My nervousness was leaving me, but I wanted so desperately to impress.

"Do you play Bach?" he asked, after.

Bach, clean, crisp, precise, *reasonable* ... stable. *Predictable* yet *un*predictable, the chromaticisms so rich, the rhythmic movement so compelling. And yet, the music failed to satisfy my soul. I worried it was evident in my playing.

"Chopin?"

"The "Minute Waltz," I announced. I'd been playing this piece of running eighths, pursuing and circling, a cat chasing its tail, since I was thirteen. Its middle section was the theme of a popular movie: *I'm always chasing rainbows....* Romantic and lyrical, it needed a singing tone and utmost *legato*. "You are a talent," he said, simply, at the end of it. "But we will have to work." He didn't say more, but I could tell from his look that he was pleased. Besides, he awarded me a grant from Settlement — and a personal scholarship, meaning I would have *two* hours a week of instruction! I was ecstatic. That it was Settlement and not Curtis could not take away from my elation. A roadblock had intruded, but not permanently obstructed my dream; instead, thanks to Mr. Filar, I made my way around it to the other side.

That was the beginning of a long arduous journey. Demanding but never cruel, he was patient. I was impatient. Full days of classes, long hours at the keyboard striving toward a perfection that would ... could ... never be reached. At the end of that year, I collapsed from exhaustion. I told myself he had survived far far harsher trials, trials that would have broken most of us. In those early days of knowing him, I saw no jaded bitterness. Only a man who had overcome, took hold and rose above. Whatever emotions he held buried during those years, he poured into the music that spoke from and to the soul. For me, he was a figure of strength, a creator of Beauty.

You will understand, then, that it was the music *and* the man I came to revere and love. Who could have known what an enormous impact he would have on my life? It was only much later that I became fully aware of his stature: *Legendary Pianist, Teacher*, read one Philadelphia review: *Fingers of gold — and a heart filled with hope and faith in the ultimate goodness of mankind.* And "The Aftenbladet," Copenhagen, Denmark: *One of the greatest living Chopin interpreters, maybe* THE *greatest!* "Arbeiterzeitung," Vienna: *Heavenly, rare, radiant ... belongs without doubt to the most fascinating pianists we have ever heard.*

A "pianist's pianist."

This is his story then, one he has kept dormant for half a century, memories too sickening to awaken. It is a story of courage, wit, fear and faith; love and loss, survival and triumph, a plague of endurance most of us can't imagine. Phantoms, shadows, that for decades peopled his dreams and nightmares haunt the looking glass when he shaves in the morning or checks the rear-view mirror in his car, rape his sleep and rise like golems from the ivories of his Steinway as he plays Chopin. The reality is that one day soon they will find no one left to trouble. All he cherished and despised, embraced and railed against, all that touched and nauseated him will die with him. When finally he admits that, when the white noise of deniers insinuates itself into public consciousness, when history's recorders implore him, that's when, summoning great courage, he agrees to ungag the words that lay unspoken on his tongue, interred in his gut, guarded in his heart; when he agrees to put a face to terrorists and torturers, victimizers and victims.

When finally he does speak, persuaded in 1994 by Spielberg's *Shoah* Foundation, Maryan Filar pries open the mammoth stone shutting in his memories, just far enough for a few to slip out: a few names here, a date there, September 1, 1939; a place, Lemberg; a texture, sister Lucy's fine wool coat and Helen's silk scarf, smooth as cream; a sound, his father Adam's booming voice; a smell, his mother Esther's brisket and onions. Once that happens there is no stopping the rush of archived recollections. Words regurgitate with the urgency of a man who at long last dares meet the reproachful eyes of the brooding living dead. Then his rage rises up from his bowels and words vomit from his lips, heaving and slapping one into the next, until all that remains is bile. Events, names, and places collide, scramble, jockey inside his brain for linear time and space, a jumble of pain and tears, fragments of memory, puzzle pieces thrown up in disarray and puked onto the floor. His rage turns to brittle determination. He will validate the ghosts of the past.

I know all this from listening to the *Shoah* tapes in the Yale library and from reading his book, *From Buchenwald to Carnegie Hall.* It tells his story: graduate of Buchenwald, Majdanek, Skarzysko Kamienna. Watching, listening to those tapes, straining to piece together his fragmented tortuous story, the *aha!* moment for me was that stunning instant when this heretofore controlled survivor dissolved in tears — the epiphanic moment when I saw, not a persona, but a person. No longer simply an unknowable icon, romanticized survivor, man of stature and reputation, but a vulnerable being with real connections, brothers, sisters, uncles, grandparents, friends; the losses suffered no longer abstractions but personal; recognizable. He started life in pre-war Warsaw, the youngest son of a comfortable, happy middle-class Jewish family. Indulged as a child prodigy, nurtured into a mature artist, he finally overcame obstacles of evil, becoming the man I am only now getting to know.

*

At age four Maryan imitates tunes his sister Helen is learning on the piano, the most glorious sounds he's ever heard. At five he is picking out themes from Mozart, Beethoven, Tchaikovsky, symphonies he's heard at concerts his mother takes him to. The astonishment when his mother and sister hear this, the joy of his father, you can't imagine. At six he begins lessons. At twelve The Warsaw Philharmonic engages him to play the Mozart D minor. By thirteen, he has outgrown the abilities of his current teacher. The great German pianist, Alfred Hoehn, hears him play Mozart and recommends he study with Professor Zbigniew Drzewiecki, the most admired musician and piano teacher in all of Poland.

One ideal July day in 1932, Maryan was on his way to his first lesson at the professor's home. He was not nervous. True, he was only fourteen, but he'd already performed with the Warsaw Philharmonic and reviews in all the newspapers were glowing: Maryan Filar, *wunderkind*, a Polish Mozart! The professor had accepted him for a summer's private study in preparation for the entrance exam to the Conservatory in September. For the whole of the streetcar ride he anticipates with an adolescent's cocky self-assurance — almost a folk idol after all! — what lies ahead.

Arriving at the professor's place — a beautiful building in the best part of the city — and on reaching Drzewiecki's apartment, he knocks at the door and is greeted by the Maestro. Esther has seen to it that Maryan is dressed in his nicest clothes, dark wool serge trousers (a recent graduation from knee pants), double-breasted jacket, starched white collar, all of which makes him look and feel somewhat formal, awkward. Drewiecki is not tall, but from Maryan's perspective the professor seems to tower above him. He has a long, pencil-thin face, with a high forehead, a pointed, prominent nose, fine broad lips and a delicate chin. Austere enough to intimidate even the most assured young man, it is his eyes, shaded and diminished by bushy brows like awnings, and a stern countenance that cracks Maryan's youthful bravado. Smoking a cigarette held between his middle and ring fingers, Drzewiecki motions without comment toward the grand; it, like the Maestro himself, dominates the room.

Maryan places his music on the piano and waits for instruction. Seated at this black solid instrument massive as a musk-ox, he seems but a boy-child, with his dark hair neatly parted and innocent eyes, ponds of cedar brown like his mother's; an adolescent in a man's upright attire. Sunbeams stream through window sheers, spilling over thick dark-velvet drapes, a plush patterned rug, imposing chests, down-filled armchairs, writing desk and framed photographs of the Maestro at the piano in his Conservatory studio, or performing with the Philharmonic in concert halls throughout Europe — all, impose a regal authority, dwarfing Maryan's slight frame. Vaguely, he conjures, wishes for, the simpler, comfortable embrace of his own home. Here his stomach flutters with uncertainty.

"What will you play?" Drzewiecki asks. He is standing beside the piano bench, slightly behind Maryan's shoulder.

"Mozart, the D minor concerto..."

"No," he interrupts. "I was *at* the Philharmonic. What else? Nevermind," with a dismissive wave of his hand. "Some scales please.... No? You don't play scales? Try," a command. "No, no, thumb *under! Under!*" He sighs. "All right then, arpeggios, chords, octaves?"

Still Maryan hesitates, his confidence deflating like a collapsed lung.

"Cramer Etudes? Kullak?"

He shakes his head.

"Do you play Bach? Scarlatti?" becoming exasperated. "What *do* you play?" Drzewiecki asks after getting no response. "Ah, yes, the Mozart concerto. You already know everything. You know *nothing!*" Drzewiecki explodes. "You believe too much the newspapers, "Focus. Discipline, *persistence*, is what you need!" still shouting.

Not used to such screaming, Maryan's insides are the quivering vibrato of a violin string; he freezes with the Maestro's look of disapproval.

"And your hand position is no good."

Maryan looks down at his small hands on the keyboard. It's the way he has always played, and these hands, after all, have taken him to the Conservatory and his first public concert at the age of six!

"Like this," the professor says and places each of Maryan's fingers in the exact centre of each key, then presses his own fingers under Maryan's palm and knuckles, forming a well-rounded arch. "Again."

By this time blinking back tears, Maryan places each finger as he saw the professor do.

"Still not," the Maestro says and readjusts each finger. "What *is* it with *this little one?*" Grabbing Maryan's pinky finger, he slams it against the keyboard.

"Ouch!"

"Knuckle out!" Drzewiecki shouts, taking Maryan's hand in his.

A knock on the door interrupts. Cigarette dangling from his lips, the professor walks over and opens it. He sees the retreating figure of Mrs. Filar and calls her back.

"I was coming to pick up my son," she says, stepping inside, "but I ... I heard shouting ... it shook *me*, I must admit. I was about to slip away...."

"I will get your son ready for the entrance exams, Mrs. Filar," he interrupts, blowing a cloud of smoke off in her direction, "but he must work. This is not the time for orchestras and appearances," he admonishes, turning to the boy, who looks like he wants to disappear into the womb of the piano. "You think you can get by on your ear and natural talent. Go, and come back when you have learned a proper hand position."

Maryan cried a lot over those summer months. Hand position, wrist position, arm weight, finger weight, *legato*, scales, chords, *arpeggios*.... In fact, he was wretched. Later, much later, he said, "Thank God Professor Drzewiecki scared the hell out of me." Later, he kept the Maestro's photograph reverently above his piano. Later, this stern master came to fill the place of the father Maryan had long ago lost. Drzewiecki is one of the intrepid ones to whom he will be forever grateful. Without them, he tells everyone throughout the rest of his life, he could not have survived.

*

Not yet fifteen — 1932 — he enters the advanced fourth level of a nine-year program at the State Conservatory of Music. He is young and full of himself. After all, he's already played with the Warsaw Philharmonic. Sounds coming from practice studios soon shake him from his perch. The most difficult virtuoso works collide, a musical collage, and resound through the halls—Liszt's *Campanella*, the Rach #3 Concerto, Beethoven's *Diabelli*, the Chopin and Brahms Concerti. The runs fast and clear, the chords powerful. Maryan reminds himself that this Conservatory is the soil of Rubinstein, Chopin, Paderewski. He gets seriously to work. Completes two years of study in one and advances immediately to the program's sixth level. Six days a week he studies piano, harmony, theory, *solfeggio*, form and analysis, all after a full day of studies at the *gymnasium*. He hears the world's finest artists perform: Rachmaninoff, Gieseking, Backhaus, Hofmann, Landowska, Rubinstein. Soon he is Professor Drzwekiecki's favourite, runs his errands, fetches his cigarettes, a coveted task amongst students.

Maryan wins first prize in the Ministry of Culture piano competitions, 1937, 1938, 1939. A scholarship of fifty zlotys a month makes him financially independent from his parents. From beggar to bourgeoisie! A capitalist!

If he wanted, he'd make a good lawyer. He has a knack for manoeuvring situations to his advantage, a certain brazen delight in taking risks. Stealing up to the second floor, with a key wheedled from a professor's son, a friend, Maryan and his companions let themselves into the back entrance of the recital hall, where they would scatter and fill the empty seats. "I'm going broke from you kids!" Max, the concert hall manager, exploding. Maryan and his friends laugh and feign surprise. Affecting contrition, with a long face and beagle eyes, Maryan would shrug and turn out the lining of his pants pockets, imploring, "You see, empty! Just enough for the streetcar home."

He thrives. At home he is surrounded by family: grandparents, cousins, aunts, and uncles. At the *gymnasium* and conservatory he is popular. The girls like him; he is nice-looking (though not stereotypically handsome), smart, talented, optimistic, and fun. Well-built, but slight, he is nevertheless good at sports (swimming and soccer); a scout troop leader.

In summer, he works on a bee farm, harvesting honey. Polish women singing in the fields strike his ears with the rhythms of the mazurka. "Chopin," he thinks. He'll play the composer's mazurkas the way the women sing. He has everything: family, friends, money, a fine education, music, his piano. Life is sunshine.

On Friday, September 1, 1939, the Germans invade Poland.

*

The day before, Thursday, was an ordinary one, ordinary as can be with the threat of war a daily companion. Maryan, his mother Esther, father Adam, sisters Helen and Lucy, brothers Joel, Michael and Ignaz, sit down to a dinner of beef soup, brisket, sweet potatoes and kasha with brown onions. The talk around the table is animated. No one talks of war.

"Play something, Ignaz," Esther urges as they are ending the meal and motions them away with a flick of her hand. "Go, go, I will finish up the dishes. Lucy will help."

"Now we are ready for some amusement," a satisfied Adam says, patting his generous girth. He pushes his chair away from the table. "Ignaz, what will we sing tonight?"

They sit themselves around the piano in the living room, as they do each evening after dinner. A golden aroma from their just-finished meal lingers; an incandescent glow warms the room; their faces; framed pictures of a young Esther and Adam; the children growing up; grandparents; a great-grandfather, a rabbi, in yarmulke and prayer shawl; Maryan, in a double-breasted jacket, breeches and leggings, the twelve-year-old posing stiffly by a concert grand, diminished by it. Middle-class Jewish, not rich, but comfortable enough. All, an amber-tinted daguerreotype of a close-knit family secure in one another, holding on to a way of life.

No one speaks of the growing background noise: fears that Germany will take Danzig and the Polish Corridor. Then, what? *All* of Poland? No longer a twelve-year-old but a young man of twenty-two, Maryan looks around at his family. These worries can't be far from everyone's mind, he thinks, recalling how the Germans grabbed the whole of Czechoslovakia after Sudetenland; why, the *Anschluss* happened only a little over a year ago.

Such was the conversation just days before, when the radio announcer reported increasing over-flights by reconnaissance aircraft. "There might yet be peace. Be patient," Adam muttered and reminded them that Poland had halted its troop mobilization; what's more, Britain and France were pushing for an agreement even now. Even now, today, as they are about to listen to Ignaz improvise on the piano after a fine dinner, the Polish Ambassador Lipsky is in Germany, negotiating with Ribbentrop. For this evening, at least, Maryan and his family will mute this background static; the radio with its news will remain silent. For these few fleeting hours, it is an ordinary evening like any other. War is still just a fear.

Ignaz begins to play. Ignaz can improvise anything. *Chryzantemy Zlociste ... Golden Chrysanthemums ...* a Poplawskiego tango about to join Poland's tango fever. "Just recorded," he tells the others. "I heard it on the radio a few days ago." He begins to sing in his nightclub tenor, "*Złote chryzantemy, w kryształowym wazonie stoją na moim fortepianie ... Golden chrysanthemums, in a crystal vase are standing on my piano....*"

By this time Esther and Lucy have come in from the kitchen. Lucy sits beside Helen on the sofa, but Adam leaps from his chair to pull his wife into a clear space in the room's centre, and with a Latin dancer's attitude and erect carriage leads her in the walking-embrace of a tango. A big man with a (gently) rounded belly, still he is light on his feet and playful; and Esther, a buxom woman, who with motherly softness fills out her girl-like flower-print blouse, is graceful, playing along with her husband. In their sixties, they are like young marrieds, a wholesome seductiveness to their easy familiarity. Maryan likes to say his mother's smile lights the world. Everyone laughs and claps, even while the words Ignaz sings are soulful: "*I reach out my hands ... and whisper ... why have you gone away?*"

"Enough," Ignaz exclaims, getting up from the piano. "Someone else's turn. Helen? Lucy? Some four-hand piano? No? Joel then." Ignaz pantomimes bowing a violin. Maryan wonders if Ignaz is purposefully overlooking him.

"He's toying with you, little brother," Michael says.

"I know," Maryan answers.

Ignaz, the joker. Michael, peacemaker.

"We all know you are everyone's pride," Helen soothes. "Play, play."

Maryan smiles at Helen, thinking again how very beautiful she is, sweet and delicate, a mimosa. He sits down at the piano, a five-foot, seven-inch Kerntopf grand his parents surprised him with when he was only twelve, and plays Chopin, the "Black Key Etude," his fingers butterflies flitting quick and light over the keys.

"You will be a great pianist one day," his mother says to him when he has finished.

He will take those words with him the rest of his life.

*

All that he loved, his family, music, the pungent smells of his mother's cooking, comforted him. Though possible, perhaps even probable, war still seemed unreal. But his life *was* real: they were fairly well-off, his father the owner of a successful wholesale clothing business down the block from where they lived on Gesia Street in a Jewish neighbourhood, and he could be home every day for lunch. True, his father had a hot-temper and when he railed at clients Michael went to the shop to smooth things over. But his father was smart and had such a laugh, the greatest anywhere. All would be the same forever.

Until the next morning, September 1. From that time on, nothing will ever be the same again.

*

Friday at five a.m. explosions violate the skies, and Maryan, standing at his bedroom window, looks out to see puffs of white smoke in the distance, coming from Polish antiaircraft shells. Soon come formations of *Luftwaffe* with their cargo of terror and destruction, flying in low, their noise and aggressive configurations like flights of hundreds of mechanized honking geese. Over the radio, Poland's President Moscicki proclaims the German attack and Poland's official state of war. Maryan bends his ear to listen as Moscicki's voice carries through the apartment; the noise of imminent war can no longer be put aside as just background static. The announcer delivers his broadcast as if it were just another day of inconsequential news.

October 1939, exactly one month after the German surprise attack on Poland, Maryan stands with his father on Wolska Street, watching the Germans marching into Warsaw. An alarming sight, they march, articulated wooden puppets, their strings manoeuvred by a mad puppeteer, their stares darts set to pierce some distant bull's eye. Listening, silent and impassive, gazing dull-eyed in the direction of the soldiers, a crowd surrounds the two of them. There is a bite in the fall air, the normally milling crowd a dark mass in their wools and twills, greys, blacks, and sombre browns. They gather now along the sidewalk: women in skirts and coats mid-calf, babushkas covering their heads, lace-up oxfords their feet; modern women, in cream coats, stylish pumps; bearded Orthodox in traditional black, their wide-brimmed hats and long frocks; Polish men casually dressed, with felt fedoras; caps, high boots and coarse tunics for pedlars hauling their carts; traders and horse-drawn wagons; businessmen in carriages, and, lined up by the side of the road, cars for the more well-to-do.

Electric trams are notable for their absence and only their tracks snaking along the middle of the cobblestone street give witness to their existence. Over all, seeming earthbound, the three- and five-storey tenements glum down on the scene below. Clothiers, haberdashers, shoe salesmen ... jewellers, tailors, apothecaries, stand under their shop awnings or in doorways, watching the parade go by, their stores emptied of customers. Nearby, the marketplace is vacant; sides of meat hang in butcher shop windows; live fish float in large trays; fresh fruit and vegetables tumble from cardboard boxes stacked on stalls. Customers gather on Wolska Avenue and blend with a disparate citizenry come together to witness the takeover of their city.

Standing alongside his father, twenty-two-year-old Maryan hears the singing of the soldiers as they approach, a unison choir and pretty good at that. A German folksong; one he *does not* know, but the sound of Germany's nationalism, of its musical giants, he *does*. Reminded of the Polish women singing mazurkas in the fields where he'd worked as a young boy, the folksongs of Poland filling the air, now, on Wolska Street in Warsaw, he hears the distinctive motifs, the rise and fall, the implied texture and harmonies, of Germany. The strength and pride.

"Tate, Tate ... Kennen ikh hern tsu vus Beethoven gehert! Father! Father, I can hear what Beethoven heard!" he cries in Yiddish. A heavy-set block of a man, Adam turns to stare at his young son. Adam's features, centred within a pie-shaped face of pale flesh embracing a bald pate, seem whittled in smooth rock, except there is a softness about his eyes and thin sensitive mouth. He shakes his head and those eyes show great sorrow. Sighing, his lips harden to resignation and resolve.

"They are coming to kill us, and my son hears Beethoven!"

*

Well, it isn't enough, is it, to march chronologically through a story, beginning to end? Every writer knows that; every reader *feels* that. An epiphany, a point toward which the narrative drives, a climax of a sort, is required: *What happens on a*

"Thursday" afternoon at four p.m.? What Thursday afternoon would you like? The day the SS wrench Maryan Filar's father, Adam, from Warsaw ghetto streets, never to be heard from again? Or the day his mother and sister vanish?

*

"Father is gone..." Maryan heard his mother, Esther, cry. He'd just returned home from work in the Ghetto, August 17, 1942. It was late, the street now eerily quiet and empty.

Gone. Period. Adam Filar, the man with the expansive sousaphonic laugh. Maryan remembered his father, tears sliding down his cheeks to blusterous glee, his laugh the loudest in the small movie house when not long ago they watched a Charlie Chaplin movie together. Next afternoon, it happened to be a Thursday, the laughter is sucked from their apartment at 172 Sienna Street; Maryan, his family, and all Jews sucked from towns and suburbs throughout Warsaw. Collected and dumped, shop owners, shoemakers, tailors, teachers, doctors, lawyers, engineers and musicians, toddlers, teenagers, the wizened old, all, thrown together in the shadows of a ten-foot-high entombing wall.

Father is gone. Esther's words resound in Maryan's head, a never-ending tune circling around a stuck needle on the phonograph. The killing trucks rumble into the ghetto that August afternoon and through the evening, blocking off street after street, grabbing Jews as if collecting chickens destined for slaughter. Except they were kinder to chickens, he thinks bitterly.

"Father was on his way to a committee meeting," Esther sobs into her son's shoulder. "A *committee* meeting. That's *all.*" Her hands and eyes implore.

He grows hot with unfamiliar stirrings of helplessness and shame. Bewildered, seeing his mother cry, this large, soft strong woman whom he has known always to hearten everyone within her embrace, stiffen confidence at any sign of weakness or doubt. Awkwardly at first, he puts his arm around her shoulders, thinking of the dreadful emptiness left by his father vanishing.

He can only imagine: his father must have been caught up with the others, who, on hearing the first low rolling growl as the trucks approached, feeling the ground agitate beneath their feet, began darting, trapped prey, rabid with the disease of imminent death. Did the Nazis, greedy for more Yids than the number snatched up by their *aktion*, their *akcja*, round up women and children from inside the buildings along the street? When caught, did they then go silently, resigned, raising their arms in surrender, their cellophaned armbands with the yellow star blending and bending like a flag at half-mast? Or did the stink of fear overtake them, their splinter-thin screams, sobs and squeals, tearing the oncoming night? Did they beat them about the head and face with the butts of their rifles? These possibilities clog his head, race across his mind's eye, each image more agonizing than the last.

"Old Mr. Naverznik," Esther cries. "Poor old Mr. Naverznik...."

His mind inflamed, he sees Naverznik, at eighty, collapsed onto his knees, his rimless specs askew, one lens smeared and cracked, his arms clasping the cleated boots of his tormentor; hears his whining, "Have mercy ... please. *Shoot me*. Let me die."

"And Mrs. Kanner? Her son?" he asks. Esther gives him an uncomprehending stare.

She needn't answer. He has heard too many of these stories, the one of the young widow Kanner and her son but a replay of so many others. He conjures the scene: pulled from their closet hiding place, she pressed the boy, just eight, tight to her belly, begging her captor to allow the child to be smuggled to a neighbour. "She's a gentile, a *Christian*," widow Kanner tried reasoning. Her captor, a Jewish policeman, a student hoping to save himself, following orders from the *Judenrat*, itself victim of threats. Loathsome commands of the Gestapo, Maryan tells himself, though this explanation was of little comfort. This policeman, this student, he might have hid the boy. Or, he thinks with revulsion, with more force than necessary sent the two to the insatiable SS.

"How many?" he asks his mother. "How many did they round up? Two hundred? Three? Four?" Esther merely shakes her head, her expression dazed.

The next day rumour spreads through the ghetto like a contagion of lice. Four hundred, he'd heard. Four hundred degraded, discarded, dehumanized beings shoved, jostled, thrown together in, what, ten trucks? They must have huddled against their enemy, not knowing what else to do. Did they soil themselves? Vomit from the reek? Weep from shame? Father must have felt the most deadly dread, the kind of fear that tears the mind to screaming bits, pieces that fly in opposing directions, desperate to break the skull's prison, a gnawing sickness deep in the well of his being.

Father gone. Saying these words to Maryan, Esther bites into her knuckles, leaving a half-circle of tooth marks, a gesture he has seen his mother do only under the most stressful instances. He struggles to absorb the meaning of "gone." Did father die in one of Warsaw's outlying forests, bludgeoned and terrorized along with the others to dig their own mortal bed of earth? Forced to strip, their nude de-sexualized bodies confirming unworthiness.

The sweet suppleness of Esther's face, her fine tulip lips and wrinkle-less cheeks, squeezed and twisted; deep brown eyes, normally serene and steady as lakes of cedar, distorted now from the effort of giving voice to the unimaginable. She grasps her son's arm, as if to draw on his young strength, and shudders, whispering — more a breathy exhaling of horror — "I *felt* it, I *knew* it, I *heard at that very instant*, the bullet *crack* ... shatter your father's head. Oh, my Adam...."

But perhaps his father hadn't died, not just then anyway. Maryan never stopped rewinding the possibilities, the words

Father gone — the unfathomable idea of it. The unspeakable thought of him transported, not to the woods but ... where? *Treblinka?* To be worked and starved to death? Or *Belzec*, where it was rumoured the Nazis turned victims' fat to soap?

Only imagine the anguish Maryan felt when he returned home, just six months later, January 1943, to find his mother Esther, and Helen, his sister, vanished, like his father. Vanished: a faded space; a cupboard once cram-packed, now empty; a phantom presence, lingering odour of cigar, toilet water, shampoo. That day, the day when his mother and sister disappeared, he came home to the sound of hollow, all the human spiritual energy siphoned off from the home that had once vibrated with sounds from the piano, guitar, violin, singing and laughter, of family arguments and chastisements and tears.

That day, when he came home to vacuous silence, he ran through the Filar apartment, in and out of its rooms, though what was the point, the place was small: *no one there.* "*Mother? Helen?*" Twenty-five, strong and lithe and quick-footed, yet at that moment he is a lost child of three, desperately screaming for his mother and sister, his futile shouts more and more frantic, met only with the echo of his own voice, "*Helen ... Helen ... Helen?*" Standing there in the living room, overcome by the realization of what had happened, suddenly grown old, he feels so crashingly alone. So empty. Emptied. For they ... *they* ... have robbed him; *they*, his fellow humans have done so. The countrymen of Bach, Beethoven, Brahms, Schumann, Schubert, Mahler. How could all have come to *this?*

No, you cannot imagine. Father, gone. Now his beloved sister and mother. His brother Ignaz and his wife Ala, stolen and sent to the ovens at *Treblinka* with their beautiful three-year-old son, Kubus, golden-haired and blue-eyed as any Hitler-approved Aryan. Maryan's brother Michael, sister Lucy and her husband Ben, packed off by the Russians to a gulag in Siberia, no more significant than carp sealed in a jar. Trapped between the Nazis and Communists. Who could have foreseen the pact between

Hitler and Stalin dividing Poland at the River Bug, the area to the east — Bialystok, Lemberg — parcelled out to the Soviets? Esther, earth mother, had been wise and prescient. Foreseeing war as early as 1935, she had managed to get her son George out of Poland and to Palestine as a safe harbour should her family need it. Only Maryan's brother Joel is left with him to face the vacant apartment on Sienna Street that afternoon. Only Joel to ease his aloneness. They will stay together through the next three years of horror.

*

Skarzysko Kamienna slave labour camp, munitions factory, Poland, 1943. Of all possible "Thursday" afternoon scenarios for this story, the story of Maryan Filar, pianist, one terrible moment eclipses all others. Just the telling shakes me in the most profound way.

Four a.m., Maryan has fallen asleep at his workbench, dreaming a nightmare. He is twenty-six, eighty pounds, skin stretched taut over protruding ribs, battered from nine weeks in Majdanek at the hands of the SS. He dreams himself back there, warehoused with hundreds of prisoners, perhaps a thousand, fifteen hundred, in a large barrack separated by a high fence from rows and rows of barracks spread over an expanse of fields the size of a small city. Barrack Number 16 gets "special treatment" deserving of Warsaw ghetto uprisers. Resting on the wooden worktable where he'd fallen asleep, a whimper sounds from his lips and his head jerks involuntarily as if being struck with the butt of a rifle. A wake-up call sounds at five a.m., so fearsome and present he can hear it even in his sleep. *Rauss! Raus Schnell!* Out! Out! *Leap* out of bed — bed, stacked rough-hewn wood planks fashioned into bunks — so many men to a shelf, crammed like cheap tuna into tins packed in a crate, that when one man shifts everyone is forced to do the same. Yes, leap, lest the judgment be a beating so brutal you will never walk again; perhaps a butt, or bullet, to the head.

In the dead of night when he goes to the latrine, he climbs out over the row of bony bodies. The men grumble, swear and threaten; grumble, swear and threaten when he rolls back in. He shivers, dreaming himself outside the barrack in early morning winter frost, the men shoeless and clothed in striped, thin cotton pyjamas. Waists slip down wasted hips; tops gape at the collar, exposing shrivelled turkey-necks and hang from shoulders gaunt and bent as wire coat hangers.

His breath quickens, heaves, a groan escapes him, and his legs, pressed against the workbench, ache with a deep remembering: running, running, desperate, ever faster; whipped onward by shouts of *Schnell! Macht schnell!*, he stumbles beneath a carried rock heavy as his body weight, for eighty, ninety, a hundred feet and back, forward and back, and again until his strength drained utterly, but he must keep on, dragging one swollen foot after the other. Men falter and fall, crushed beneath the burden, their last breath squeezed from them.

Those still standing march the rest of the day, march to nowhere, march for miles to no purpose, no end; march until they collapse. *Auf! Auf!* — their tormentors snarl. He understands even in his slumber: *They do not want us to work; they want us to die.* A sharp clap, a *pop!* — a shot so final it has no after-life — splits the air. His shoe worn thin and cracked, he feels something warm and sticky seep through its sole; matter splays onto the bottom of his pyjama pants. An inmate lies on the ground, dead as stone. Blood from a stone. Polished black boots of the SS straddle the useless figure. They loom, obliterating his vision. But the shot of his dream is the thud of a club against his skull, the boots those of a guard by his side. *Auf! Auf!* jolts him out of one nightmare and into another. The blow knocks him forward, thrusting his left hand into the knife he'd fallen asleep holding in his right — a knife to cut parts for machine guns. You cut a thing in half to make two parts, but he is too used up to understand. He just does what they tell him.

An acute searing pain grips him. Lightning streaks up his hand and arm, so hot and sharp he is blinded by it. Red mist clouds his eyes. Blood gushes from his index finger, colours his hand red, stains the wood beneath it, drips through cracks, wets his thigh and drips onto the floor. He struggles to clear his vision but can make out only his bloodied hand and sliced finger. *"Helfen sie mir!"* he pleads. *"Ich verliere meine finger von der Infektion. I will lose my finger from infection."*

"Sie wird erschossen. You will be shot! Sie wierden nutzlos für uns. Useless to us."

Maryan sobs, not from pain, an agony his body has come to own now, but from utter despairing powerlessness. Hate and rage devour him as he glares vacant-eyed at the guard, terrifying in his jackboots and grey uniform, thick black belt, gun holster and whipping cane at his side; the silver eagle on his cap, swastika armband, blurs, the grinning *totenkopf* above the brim mocking him with death. Terrifying in his grotesqueness, this Nazi sadist, this piece of human shit, this misshapen hunchback stuffed in his dwarf-like body, has a sprinkle of cake crumbs on his lapel. Even in his groggy state, seeing hazily out of his half-lidded eye, Maryan notes this detail. His right hand tightens around the blade handle. *What do I have to lose? He will kill me anyway. I am no good to them now. Go to hell!* Their eyes meet, the Nazi's cold and daring: *Hab ich dich, Jude! I have got you, Jew!* But Maryan has no strength; his arm goes limp, slackens.

"Eine weitere nutzlose Jude! Another worthless Jew! the guard mutters, a disdainful guttural grunt. He spits and turns on his heels, leaving Maryan in mental agony.

*

How does one survive these terrors and not lose one's senses? *Buchenwald. Skarzysko Kamienna. Majdanek.* Maryan's music carried him through, even when, during his three years in the camps, he could not play, could hear no great orchestras, no chamber music, no artists, Gillels, Hofmann, Horowitz, no Rubinstein nor Rachmaninoff; when he had only the music in his soul. When there was no God, there was God's splendour. Only music kept him from becoming slave to the devil of bitterness, hate, and despair.

He would never know what happened to his mother, father, and sister Helen. He'd lost forever his brother Ignaz, his sister-in-law Ala, and nephew Kubus; only later, after the war, would he find out the fate of his brother Michael, sister Lucy, and her husband Ben.

*

It was decades since I had studied with Mr. Filar, 1952, and I was determined to find out where he was living and reconnect with him once again. After all, this year, 2009, he would be 92. How many chances to meet with him would I have? Although I'd kept in touch over the years, today I'm seeing him for the first time after a long stretch.

"Do you play anymore? Will you play something?" I ask, and immediately regret my request. In his Philadelphia retirement apartment — actually two joined to make one large — he's seated on one end of the piano stool, a sheepish smile on his lips, looking at me, standing beside the Steinway and facing him. At ninety-two, his once agile hands are fleshy and bent from arthritis. He reaches over to the keyboard and with three fingers manages a *diddle-diddle-diddle*, then shrugs as if to say, "There you have it."

"They just sent me the Polish editions of the Chopin. Have a look, they're on the couch," he said earlier that afternoon when I first arrived. He must have noted my blank stare because he repeated himself. "The Polish editions, the Paderewski for me to try out. They sent them. The German ones are lousy."

Over the years, he has taken to speaking a colloquial English, the voice he uses in his book, published in 2002, seven years back. Coupled with a hint of a foreign syntax and laden with cliché, the use of such common language from a man who speaks seven languages fluently offends my ears, like bad playing; a man who once painted word-pictures, pure poetry, of the music he wanted to flow through my fingers. Debussy *... dewdrops at sunrise ... raindrops deep inside a fir-green forest ...* Schumann *... the baby sleeps, gently rocks, see its lashes flutter, its rose-lips, how they purse....*

"Polish editions?" My question showed my bewilderment. He pointed out these same editions some years ago on a previous visit. That was when he lived in a spacious apartment off fashionable Rittenhouse Square. Now, now he's in a place the name of which he can't remember, a place of no address, at least none he can recall. "I'm in a retirement home," he had said over the phone earlier. "Wait, I'll ask its name. Wait, I'll ask where it is. Wait, I'll.... Wait. Call me back."

Each time I called back it was the same. Finally he stopped answering, and not knowing what else to do I left a message. Eventually, I did some sleuthing and tracked down the place.

Still seated at the piano, he appears to be waiting for me to say something, though perhaps, Maryan Filar, protégé of the great Gieseking, is simply bewildered by his own inertia; his idle, stiff fingers that had managed only a *diddle-diddle*, the now-silent keyboard.

I glance up at framed photos on the wall beside the Steinway, of him playing under Leinsdorf, Ormandy and Kubelik, of letters from Rubinstein and Gieseking. They act as stimulants to his memory, reminders of happier times, after the war. Along with the grand piano, they dominate the small living room. A photograph shows him with a group of his students, taken many years ago, myself among them. He's lean, and even from the photograph one can feel the strength, the stiffness of spine to his character. I remember how centred he was, how his self-assurance — a calmness that comes with being comfortable in one's own being — made him appear taller than his actual short stature. At the same time, I remember his intensity, which seemed to spring from that core; how he seemed always prepared to move forward, take charge. Now there's an uncharacteristic slackness; he has become shorter, round and fleshy, though not fat; "soft" seems fitting. There's an innocence about him, a childlike trust, inconceivable considering his history.

Looking at that photograph so long after it was taken, I'm conscious of how his life at different points in time has glanced off my own, bouncing from impact to impact like a tumbling fragment of angled rock, leaving its mark with each encounter. I wonder if he's aware how deep — if at all.

Across the bottom of Gieseking's photo is the German pianist's autograph: *to Maryan, my dear friend and protégé.* There is Maryan in another photo, shaking hands with famed conductor Kubelik. Artur Rubinstein: *to Maryan, the finest interpreter of Chopin.* A framed letter, written in Gieseking's hand, introduces Maryan to *my music colleagues in the United States* and attests to the *awesome talent of this remarkable musician.*

He and I have moved to sit beside one another on the sofa, where we quietly reminisce about those things he does remember and those I help him to. I take his hand in mine. It's soft and plump beneath my fingers, white as cream of wheat but for a sprinkling of light brown spots that are more like adolescent freckles than a symptom of age; his nails, well-manicured. I can't help but compare it with those in the photograph on the wall, between that of Gieseking and Kubelek, the one taken many years back of Maryan's hands resting on the keyboard: fingers slender, elongated, palms and knuckles arched, their span and that of his fingers wide, the hands themselves lean and strong. Now, his resigned flesh is metaphor for the man's new compliancy, allowing me to hold his hand as though *I* were the wise mentor.

I refer to him here as "Maryan," but really, I've never been able to call him anything but *Mr. Filar.* I never understood why, especially as we grew older and the gap of years between us became meaningless. The few times I tried calling him by his first name, I sensed he wasn't pleased, though he said nothing. Not until after I'd read his book did I recognize the cultural difference, the North American penchant for familiarity, the European for regard. Even when, as an inmate, a slave, stripped of all that gives meaning to one's life, when all social graces had been shed and correctness didn't matter, even then, in letters smuggled out of the camp, he addressed his Conservatory teacher as *Professor* and *Maestro*. And later, when he was freed, when he established himself in his own right as *Professor* and *Maestro*, even then I never heard him confer a lesser title, such high regard did he have of teaching. Gieseking was *Maestro* Gieseking, never Walter. *Walter* would have been unthinkable.

I think it must be that even now, "grown-up" and "a woman" — past middle-age at that — the same ever-conscious regard I had for him when I was a young girl keeps me from the easy familiarity of the American way

"This is an old scar," I say, stroking his index finger, bringing his attention to it.

"Yes, it happened in...." He turns a blank stare to meet my gaze. "I don't remember where it happened. I almost didn't play again."

"You almost severed the nerve. An inmate helped you, a doctor, remember? I think his name was Dov. 'You will never play the piano again,' he told you. But then he got an idea: '*Calium hypermaganicum*. Crystals, immersed in hot water, turns the water blue-purple. Get some.'"

Civilian Polish workers at Skarysko Kamienna were a lifeline to the outside world and Maryan learned to use every bit of cunning, every intuition of human psychology to shape his own fate, even when the slightest error or betrayal meant death. He'd persuaded a sympathetic Polish civilian factory overseer to secret the disinfectant to him, he recounts in his memoir; persuaded with money collected from his Conservatory colleagues and Professor Zbigniew Drzewiecki, then smuggled in. It was months of agonizing before the swelling began to subside and when it did he "practised" on a wooden table, striking it as if depressing keys of a piano. "Such relief, you cannot imagine." (Maryan's words, when some feeling had begun to return to the injured digit.) Hope, faith in a future, and the deep wellspring of music in the core of his soul — his *need* to create — were, after all, what would see him through the horror.

"I will have to read about it in my book," he says, after I explain how he recovered. I'm again taken aback by the innocence of his statement, its candour, his humble, clear-eyed acceptance.

He has the same simple trusting persona about him as he did earlier this afternoon when I entered the apartment after waiting for what seemed a half an hour before he opened the door, quite unlike the punctual, purposeful, quick-footed man I once knew. "Just a minute, I'm coming," and "I'll be there soon," and "Give me three minutes," he called, intermittently, while I waited outside his door. "So sorry I'm late," I offered when finally he let me in. "I got lost and..."

"It doesn't matter," he said, with a dismissive wave. "I was taking a nap." He did, in fact, look as if he'd just stumbled out of bed. His thinning hair uncharacteristically dishevelled, his grey loose-fitting track pants, open-collar, short-sleeve, plaid shirt redolent of a retired used-clothing storeowner in South Philadelphia in the fifties. I'm surprised at the short sleeves. I expected to see numbers branded on his arm. Perhaps I missed seeing them. What looked to be a food stain, set by many washings, discoloured the plaid stripes down the shirtfront. This last distressed me. Still, there was nothing dishevelled or bedraggled about his mood. "I was sleeping. We had a big party last night until two in the morning."

"Two? Here? How come you stayed out so late?"

"I was having a good time!"

I laughed at the simplicity of his answer. That all happened earlier this afternoon, the tone light-hearted. He seems more settled now, but has the same air of submission, of yielding about him. The vitality I remember of yesteryear has been replaced with the unhurried contentment of someone with nothing to prove, no appointments to keep, no ego to satisfy. No memories to press on him.

"You know," I say aloud, continuing our conversation about the camps, still stroking his hand, "My grandfather's sister Sura wrote to him in America, letters — they run from, oh, 1933 to '39.... *We are desperate ... the situation hopeless ...* in Yiddish, in Polish — from Lwow ... Lemberg back then..."

"Lemberg," he interrupts. His eyes take on a distant searching, a quick flash of recognition. "I know that city. I was there. Now why was I there? Why did I go?" He turns to me, as if I could provide the answer.

"You fled Warsaw when the Germans entered." I continue to fill in for him the history that no longer burdens his memory: "You went to Bialystok — to help with the resistance. Then to Lemberg. Do you remember? Your conservatory teacher had left Warsaw for there by that time and you were hoping to study with him again? Life went on," I say ruefully, knowing he must at some level still comprehend that more than I.

"How do you know why I went?"

"Your book," I smiled.

"You read it? All of it? You bought it?"

"Indeed." I reach over to the coffee table and retrieve the book from my briefcase. "Will you sign it for me?"

He is like a child in his delight. I hand him a pen and slip of paper on which I'd written in large caps my name, sure that he will have forgotten it. I watch as he laboriously, in a shaky hand, autographs the title page: *To Rhoda ...* (signed) *the author, Maryan Filar. Best wishes. November 2009* (he asks for the date).

The skeletal bareness of the engraving, its minimalism, like scraping the bone, pains me perhaps more than anything he has said this day. It is not anything this dear man has written that causes such a pang, such a feeling of void in that place wherever such sadness resides, but any expression of familiarity, fondness or shared memories, so glaringly missing from the script.

"Lemberg," I say to bring him back on track. He lays the pen down and turns once more to me.

"My book..." he says.

He will have to read his book to remember what happened in Lemberg. To find out about his life.

"Yes, I married a woman in Lemberg, but I.... She was from Brazil."

"I think you're remembering the woman you married when you were living in Philly, long after the war," I prompted. "You were already teaching, playing concerts with Ormandy and the Philadelphia Orchestra, the Cleveland Symphony, the New York Philharmonic..."

"I married a woman in Philadelphia?"

"From Brazil."

"She was from Brazil?"

"Yes."

"It must have been the same woman as from Lemberg."

I don't disabuse him of this, but steer the conversation away from the confusion over Lemberg and the woman he married and divorced not long after the wedding. "She wanted a babysitter, not a husband," he once told me; wanted him to leave Philadelphia for Brazil. "And she said she didn't smoke. She did. Who wants to be married to a smoker and a liar?" (He wrote only nice things about her in his memoir.)

"Do you remember I was your very first student in America?" I see that he doesn't; he's looking at me with keen interest. "Yes, and you gave me a scholarship for two hours a week."

"*Two* hours? Really? I'm impressed."

"I was a very serious student. You used to make a joke: I reminded you of a man you knew in the camps. Like you —

we'll call him Nathan — he couldn't have weighed more than eighty pounds. It was at the end of the war and the allies were within a few miles of the camp. It meant liberation. "*Oy vey, oy vey!* What will I do when I'm free?" And you wrung your hands in imitation and laughed."

"I said that?" Maryan asks, looking thoroughly delighted with himself.

"Yep. This little story of 'Nathan' carries the finest traditions of Yiddish *kvetching*! Speaking of survival, what happened to your brother who managed to stay with you through Buchenwald, Majdanek, and Skarzysko Kamienna?"

I spell out these horror mills, not certain how many names he can recall. Perhaps he'll have to reread his book, I smile to myself.

"Michael?" he asks, but I remember that the brother in question was called Joel. "Michael?" he repeats. "Is he still alive? I ... I don't know. Why don't I know? I can't remember. He was strong, you know. Tough. He could beat any Nazi, no matter how big."

"You're remembering your brother George, I think. The strong one." I remind him that Esther had sent George to Palestine early on. "I believe it was Joel who was by your side in the camps. Michael and Joel came with you to the United States. Lucy and Ben settled in Palestine," I add. Miraculously (for who understands these things?), Maryan and Joel caught sight of Michael, Lucy and her husband Ben in Lodz after the war.

"You know that?" he asks.

"They survived the gulag. It's in your book."

"Now, why can't I remember if Joel is still alive?" he murmurs to himself.

Then he wanders off in a different direction, digging down into a reservoir of experiences that have wondrously survived his massive forgetting. Experiences saturated with the music that provided him with the constancy of meaning. He asks, with full comprehension, what I did after I left his mentorship, who did I study with, what did I learn, did I have a good teacher and was he a fine musician?

"Yes, very fine," I answer. "But you were the best Chopin interpreter and teacher. Everything I ever learned about playing, anything worthy of my effort, really, I learned first from you. 'The difference between a good performance and a fine one is in attention to the details.' Just one of many insights you gifted to me."

"But of course, that is true, what I taught you. I had two wonderful teachers. They influenced my life. My professor at the Warsaw Conservatory, Professor Zbigniew Drzewiecki and Gieseking."

His gaze slides over to the wall opposite, to the photograph of the great German pianist. Maryan's entire mien has changed with the recollection. He looks younger, refreshed, his seated posture straightened, his focus sharpened. A hint of the strength of the man has taken over, reminding me of what I yearn for him to be again.

"I played Chopin better than the Maestro," he says, somewhat abashedly, "but his Debussy! Oh, there was nothing like it. He was amazing! Unbelievable!" As with so many of Maryan's expressions, coupled with his Polish accent, these superlatives strike my ear as out of true, like wallpaper seams hung without benefit of a plumb line.

"After the war, you know, I travelled to Vienna. I asked everyone, even the man on the street, where could I find the best piano teacher in Germany. I *had* to study. Years in the camps had robbed me. Weisbaden, the great Gieseking lived in Weisbaden. A spa, I found out."

I marvel privately at the ease with which he recalls the name of the town and its renown as a place of healing.

"I took the train and found his villa, a beautiful home, very large, like an estate. He was very wealthy. I knocked on the door and Gieseking himself answered. I asked to play for him and he was very kind, very nice. He let me in, and I played.

'Why do you want to study with me when you can play Chopin like that?' he asked. 'I want to. I need to,' I told him. I studied with him for the next five years."

But I remember he'd recounted (many times) a quite different story years back, when I was his student in Philadelphia: *"I took the train and found where he was living in Weisbaden. I knocked and when the Maestro answered, told him what I wanted. 'Nein,' he said and moved to close the door. 'Du schuldest mir.... You owe me,' I said and forced my foot between the door and the frame. He was accused by many of being a Nazi collaborator—you see, he stayed in Germany and performed when so many other artists left—nobody knew for sure, so he lived away from the city, almost in seclusion, and he was very poor by then and had little to eat. Because he was proud and didn't want to take anything, I used to sneak bread in and hide it in the piano, under the lid, or on the windowsills behind the curtains."*

He has no recollection of a poor Gieseking refusing him entry or of telling me the version I recall. He insists my iteration is inaccurate and my memory must be failing me. And, the Maestro was no Nazi collaborator, he insists. A few minutes later, he tells me the Gieseking story again, of his wealthy villa, his kind welcome, the injustice of the accusations. After the fourth or fifth retelling, I figure it's time to say goodbye.

"Are you still playing?" he asks as I gather up my things. He seems somewhat surprised, confused that I'm leaving.

"No, but I did for a long time. After recovering from the brief meltdown I had while studying with you, trying so hard to measure up, I was more determined than ever. But I'm writing now. Fiction." I laugh. "I can no longer separate what I've made up from what really happened."

I linger a while, telling him about the published stories, the novel. He seems deeply interested and asks what it is about, its plot, is it autobiographical, and finally, with a conspiratorial air, "And is there a musician in the book?"

"Always," I reply. "Always a pianist and a beloved teacher. Always."

*

"*Mr. Filar, it's Rhoda calling. I just left your place. We talked about Lemberg and Gieseking and you signed your book for me. Do you remember? You must get someone to come and erase the message I left early this morning before I came to see you.*"

"*You left a message?*"

"*Yes, you keep hearing the same one and seeing the same caller* ID *and trying to call me back. You must erase it.*"

"*I'll tell someone.*"

"*I'll be in touch. So you won't forget me.*"

"*Rhoda. Yes, Rhoda. You said I was the best teacher.*"

"*I did. And you were. I'm going to miss you.*"

"*Then you'll come once a month and I'll give you a lesson!*"

Later, reflecting on the day, I tell myself how very precious these last hours have been. Who would have thought back then when I was a young woman studying with him, the master teacher, acclaimed Chopin interpreter, with his diplomas from the Warsaw Conservatory, Buchenwald, Majdanek, Skarzysko Kamienna, protégé of the unmatched Walter Gieseking, that the most touching relationship with Maryan Filar, the man, would come a half century later?

Back then I did not know the man behind the assumed persona; he revealed so little. I didn't know how much daring, courage, street-smart quickness of wit made up his character. I would discover that only gradually, after viewing the Shoah tapes and now, when his book tells his full story. Back then, I could not imagine him outside the piano studio, couldn't place him in a context, not even within a family, like the rest of us ordinary people; couldn't imagine him with sisters and brothers or girlfriends.

Growing up in Poland, did he live in a house with massive

sideboards, overstuffed sofa and easy chairs? Or an apartment, perhaps with sleeker Bauhaus designs? Was his father a doctor? Professor? Simple *shmatteh* merchant? (He was.) Were they religious or secular? His grandfather might have been a rabbi. His mother would have kept kosher. I wonder if he liked Polish pirogues, brisket and *barszcz* (borscht). Perhaps they had prints or watercolours hanging from their walls. Then again, Maryan might have lived with no art at all, just framed sepia photographs of ancestors; his parents; himself performing as a child prodigy.

Did his family live in a largely Jewish neighbourhood, or a Jewish *quarter*? On a quiet middle-class street? Or on one bustling with activity and aggressive, haggling shop merchants, like South Street in south Philadelphia in the days when I was growing up? For what did I know then of economic and societal circumstances of Jews in pre-war Poland?

Despite his reserve, his strength and self-assurance, his deep brown eyes and sensitive mouth gave him away, communicated his humanity. He was demanding. I don't remember *ever* getting a compliment from him about my playing; only once, when it came round-about by way of a parent of another student — but never cutting, never devastating or demeaning like some great artist teachers. I think I was in love with him for those qualities. Well, not only. The very reserve that kept him a mystery fed the romance of my imaginings. Throw in a large measure of awe, of the artist whose Chopin carried into the conservatory halls as I ran up the steps to his studio and opened the door, oh so quietly, and took an unobtrusive seat, allowing him to finish. His focus never wavered. He never looked up until the last sound grew too faint for the ear.

Occasionally, standing behind me as I sat at the piano bench, he'd lightly place his hand on my back (or hair; am I imagining that?) and say, "You have on a lovely perfume today, Rhoda," but nothing inappropriate. Nothing that crossed the line between student and teacher. Nothing more than a casual acknowledgment. Still, I never offered any cues for it to become more. I told myself he was seventeen years older than I, believing family and social morés prevented me from leaving the secure boundaries of the piano bench. Whatever feelings I had were contained by an ever-conscious awareness of the divide between student and master teacher, like a guarded de-militarized zone, which one dared not cross. Probably a good thing, since, man of honour that he was, I do not believe he would ever have broken that trust. Many, many years later I reconnected with him. "Rhoda!" he exclaimed when first hearing my voice over the phone. "Of course I remember you.... *I always loved you!*" Now you can interpret this in any number of ways, but I can't help reflect on the irony, on lost possibilities.

Ironic, how the sum — richness — of one's life lives within memory's palm, how it has come to abandon him. I ask myself, why should he remember the awed student desperate to please: scales and arpeggios, repetitions and frustrations, doubts and confusions, tribulations and triumphs? All those hours in the studio, days, months, years, lifetimes ago, are become but splinters of time. And yet, *this*, I think, is the epiphanic moment of *my* narrative, not the conventional orgiastic male arc perhaps, but this intimate quiet catharsis, when he has no memory of me or of his demanding instruction, his insistence on just the right timbre, most delicate *pianissisimo*, driving crescendo, thunderous *fortissimo*, most silken *legato*. Ironic that only now do I feel an intimacy I never dreamed could be.

After surviving starvation, infection, dysentery and typhoid, humiliation and horror; after glorying in the genius of Beethoven and Brahms and Schumann; after earning the admiration of Gieseking, Ormandy, Kubelek and Szell, Maryan Filar lives out his days unable to remember the name of his closest, dearest, Holocaust-surviving brother, or whether that brother is still living.

But he's happy, spared the torment of some whose memories relive, with the same intensity of old, the unrelivable, their nights sleepless or riven with dreaming and re-dreaming the nightmare, their days troubled by the approach of night. Maryan, my Professor Filar, hangs onto his crystal shards, selective memories, his Gieseking glory, his Chopin *arabesques* and *cadenzas*.

So much of his life has disappeared, vanished. Where? I want to think the lost but divine memories have flown up to that starry cosmos where Kabbalists believe scattered sparks of enlightenment will once again be united, where this fractured, suffering universe will be made whole. As for rediscovering those who were part of who he was and is, those calling his name, mystically channelling him through light-years, whispering "remember us," and "remember when," and "remember the time;" who, brushing his back with a gossamer touch light as a Mozart melody, stir in him a ghostly sense of their presence, well, as for them, he'll find them in his book.

Author's Note: Research and my imagination put flesh on the bones of accounts of Mr. Filar's life in Poland before the War and in the Nazi camps and helped me fill in gaps where I could not possibly have had first-hand knowledge. I studied with Maryan Filar — newly arrived in the United States — in Philadelphia in the fifties. Real-life facts, a few snippets of Mr. Filar's remembered accounts of dialogue, and events, have been gathered from descriptions told to me by him over the years, from the taped interview he gave for the Spielberg Shoah Foundation archives at Yale University in 1994, and from his book, From Buchenwald to Carnegie Hall, co-written with Charles Patterson in 2002. And, of course, from my visit with him in his retirement home in 2009. Maryan Filar died at the age of 95, in Philadelphia in 2012, having succumbed to advanced Alzheimer's.

Aspects of Nature

DINNER IS A FORMAL AFFAIR. Roger and Carrie have always insisted on this propriety, city or country. Surrounded by water, woods, scrub-grass and wildflowers, a path, and massive boulders leading down to the lake, it's an imposing frame-and-stone two-storey number. They call it a cottage. It's a Canadian thing.

Except for our hosts, everyone is here for the weekend as singles: David, a Trinidadian, mid-twenties, wonderfully good-looking with smooth mocha skin, curly black hair, and a gold-loop in each ear, apprentice with Ernst and Young, accountants, Roger's training him; platinum-blonde Elana, real-estate agent, in her fifties but a knock-out; Peter, divorced, a tough-talking, macho, Elmore Leonard Glitz-type, marshmallow underneath I suspect; and Jan, divorced, early forties pushing mid-, teacher turned student-lawyer. Wants her life neatly arranged in a slender leather briefcase, she's tired of chaotic and messy carried in large totes the way educators do. Sparring friends, she and Pete are forever going at each other. But for David, we've all known each other for years.

"Has anyone asked Rog why he has only half a beard?" I whisper to platinum Elana, seated to my right.

"We're not noticing," Elana whispers back.

I ask the same question of David to my left. David smiles and shrugs.

This question's been plaguing me since Roger picked me up

earlier this afternoon in his speedboat at the dock on Resolution Bay. As he approached, I sensed something off-kilter, out-of-whack. He was shockingly gaunt, wrists gangly, khakis slipped down around his hips, turkey-neck rising out of his cotton crew, but no, something else was off-centre.

A deep tan from the past summer — the only healthy aspect about him — gave his face a smooth modelled look, his hair extraordinarily black. (Is he dyeing it?) As he took my duffel and planted a peck on my lips, I felt stubble scratch against my jaw and noticed dark, porcupiney hairs covering only half the beard area, right side of his face to mid-chin.

I pretended not to notice.

"Has anyone asked why Roger has only half a beard?" I ask Janet and Peter across the table from me (Carrie and Roger have gone into the kitchen; still, I keep my voice low).

"Who the hell knows with Roger?" Peter, Mister Macho, answers in his baritone-twang. "He's got his reasons I guess."

I wasn't going to get a sensible answer from Peter, I should have known that. I ask anyway. I guess it's the writer in me.

"What? What reasons?"

Outside, the water whips under the moon's light, evergreens bend beneath singing winds, and rain, beating maracas, hits against the windows. Distant thunder groans, swells, an organ, lightning slashes. Inside, sitting primly in dress clothes under candle-glow around a fastidiously set table, we're at odds with the storm, lake, dark woods, moonlight.

"Natural's over-rated *I* say," Jan's remarking to Elana; she nods approval of Elana's bleached coiffure.

"Me too," Roger cuts in, smiling. (He and Carrie have returned.) He's regained his health, dressed in a navy double-breasted blazer, his half-beard like a mustard spot on his freshly laundered shirt, robin-egg blue. He sits down at the head of the table — close by Elana — Carrie at the opposite end.

Everyone's eyes are focused on his chin.

Perhaps he's posing some philosophic question: *If a tree falls in a forest…? Is the glass half full or half empty?* Is Roger's beard half grown in or half shaved off?

"*Highly* over-rated," Jan carries on. "Why would I want to look my age?" (pointedly) to me. *Her* hair is vibrant aubergine.

"Just tell everyone you're ten years *older*, they say '*Really?* You look great!'" I answer.

"This is a dumb conversation," Peter interjects (that private-eye twang again).

"What do *you* know, Pete?" Jan shoots at him."

"Harvey never liked it if I didn't look just so," Elana says. Her gaze embraces Roger. "Neither did Matthew. Sam wasn't so fussy. My husbands," she informs young David. "Harvey committed suicide, Matthew I divorced, and Sam … I adored Sam and he adored me. Our marriage was a love affair, a long magnificent affair. Ask Roger. You knew the way we were, didn't you, Rog?" She leans in, touches his hand lightly, momentarily; innocently, that's its wallop.

"Ta, sweetheart," Roger answers as innocently.

"Is nobody gonna ask Roger why he's shaved only half his face?" Peter asks.

The question asserts itself like the bite of an oboe; our voices drop *sotto voce* and I catch a few sidewise peeks in Roger's direction. If he's heard he doesn't let on (except for a little smile that plays around his lips).

"Roger's the only one, he's been such a dear," Elana tells me in her mauve-velvet voice.

This last bit of conversation floats above the table, hangs there, capturing Roger's wife, Carrie's, ear. The others tune in. She turns from Peter, levels her gaze on Elana, her platinum-blonde by the candles' flames crème caramel.

"Buying a hard-leather, slim — read *power* — briefcase, making changes," Jan, says, trying to pull the conversation back. Her green eyes shine uncommonly bright; her skin appears recently facialed, brows precisely arched; flat chested as a ballerina, no bum, no hips; sharp-edged, gutsy, with-it.

"I'm thinking of getting an earring," Roger tells me, smiling, his eyes on David. They drink in David's milk-chocolate complexion, delicious black curls. "To go with my gold chain." (Is he putting me on?)

David's very quiet, very shy. Candlelight glances off the gold loops; they glint. I admire his daring, not one loop, *two*, one in each ear. Catching David's eye and still smiling, Rog gives him a long slow wink. (Is he putting us *all* on?) He's become very natty lately, on the style-edge, taken to wearing a black fedora, raked; locked the Corporate Accountant away in a closet.

"Wha'ja shave half your face for, Rog?" Pete insists, hardly above a whisper, but we all hear him. "You gonna let us in?"

Not by the hair of his chinny-chin-chin!

"No reason," Roger laughs, "None."

"Bullshit!" Pete throws at him, raising his voice. The wine's gotten to Pete, its heat and the red of his sweater — he's dressed more casually than the rest of us tonight — have given his cheeks a cherubic glow.

(Maybe he has follicle disease and only one side grew in, how do we know?)

"When there's been nobody, I could always count on Roger," Elana says, ignoring Peter. "So unusual for a man. We've known each other since we were children. Be a darling, Roger, and pour me some wine?"

Carrie's been talking to David, nose to nose, but I catch her shooting quick surreptitious glances down the table's length at her half-bearded husband. She's a pet white-mouse: tiny pale face; poodly mess of mousey ash-blonde; thin lips, teeth even and slightly forward, narrow chin, pointed, receding; small nose, warm brown eyes.

Now she gets up, walks purposefully into the kitchen and moments later returns with a large bowl of soup, cold carrot. (I think she chose it as colour contrast to her black hostess gown.) Pet mouse or no, Carrie is long and flat-chested like

Jan, with no excess of curve or flesh; has a flair for the dramatic, looks smashing, sexy in asexual mode.

"Sam died suddenly ... when ... when...," Elana demurely lowers her eyes, lightly touches her hand to the platinum wave at her temple.

"Soup, Elana dear?" Carrie asks, standing beside her.

As she moves in to the table, Carrie catches her foot on the hem of her gown, is momentarily jolted, and as she looks down, her soup-spoon arm bends with the rest of her body, tipping the ladle.

"Carrie!" Roger shouts, "Watch what you're doing, you almost got Elana!"

"Yes, so I did," slight nervous giggle, "Oh, dear!"

Elana smiles good-humouredly. "You would!" she kids, fingering the gold Peretti heart on the velvet band at her neck. "You've always envied me in my white chiffon!"

Carrie's eyes take in dress, hair, back to dress. Elana's roots show a quarter-inch of dark against Madonna-blonde, other than that she's perfection. I've never seen her caught exposed before. It jars like Roger's half-beard, forces you to view reality from a new perspective, a Picasso.

Carrie dips the ladle, her arm trembles, moves toward Elana's shoulder, balancing. We all watch. The room shines like sunrise — crystal, candles, nubbly silverware, fire; outside, lightning — the ladle nears the plate and suddenly Elana's white chiffon has great orange flowers decorating its front. No sound comes from her; she only stares straight ahead, her eyes very wide. Drumroll of thunder. Serving wine, Roger's arm freezes mid-air; Carrie's little mouse-face twitches and a weak squeal escapes. We all stare at the orange blobs.

Very slowly Elana turns to Carrie.

"You always disliked me," Elana whispers.

"Roger, get Elana a towel, don't just sit there," Carrie, sharply to her husband. "Do something, move your beard ... *body!*" correcting herself.

"You were jealous," Elana says matter-of-factly. "Jealous of me and Sam."

"Elana, you're crazy," Carrie says.

"Of what we had," Elana persists.

"You must get those roots touched," aubergine-haired Janet interrupts.

"Try a different colour," Pete mumbles. He's glazed now, "What ya got doesn't go with orange."

Roger's returned and is towelling Elana's front.

"Oh stop, Roger!" she shouts, getting up, and reaching back, yanks down her zipper, gives a little shake, a wiggle, and the dress slips to her ankles.

Elana stands regally before us in oyster satin panties and bustier, garters holding up shimmery stockings. The aslant Peretti dangles from its white velvet band, teases.

Ever the polite Trinidadian, David, without a word, helps Elana step over the dress and picks it up off the floor. He lays the dress gently over the back of the chair, then offers Elana his arm to leave the room, but turning from him, she plunks back down.

"Wine?" Roger asks.

"I'll take my soup in a plate, please," Elana counters, ice.

Wind rattles the panes and whistles down the chimney, lightning forks, rends the sky, pulses one two, a strobe; cymbals clash, drums rumble, candle-glow quivers in a flame-dance. Except for Elana, we shudder and look out at the rain still thrumming against the windows. It fills the silence.

Elana wears a size 38D.

Out of the corners of my eyes I see everyone lost deep in Elana's crevice, the bustier cupping, making molehills into mountains.

"So where were we?" Roger asks.

Carrie's taken her place at the table and keeps her eyes on Roger. I'm not certain whether to stare at beard or boobs.

"How's the stock market doin', Pete?" Roger asks.

"Up and down, hot right now," Pete answers; he seems to have backed off his needling. "Bullish."

"I asked you about the *stock market*," Roger quips.

"I ask you again: Why would I — why would *anyone* want to look their age?" Jan's green eyes challenge me. "Listen, I meet my own girls at the university. Melanie's nineteen you know, and Barbie's twenty-one. I even bump into Pete's two. You don't know what it's like keeping up with young kids. All you worry about, Jan, is your computer."

"The ultimate in control, working alone," I grant.

"You did this on purpose Carrie," a small voice from Elana.

"Try getting a job with grey," Jan continues. "Try getting a decent guy. Life's competitive out there."

"Don't worry, Jan, in the dark, grey goes to black with everything else," Pete jumps in; his acerbic edge says he's had it with Jan's talk.

"Look, I'm not searching for anyone. Once was enough," Jan, to Peter.

"Did you know our Ashley's going to France next year? The Sorbonne," Carrie, back to playing hostess, is saying to anyone who'll listen, "And Fred's entering M.I.T."

"We don't want them setting their sights too high," Roger grins.

"Did you buy the Cineplex stock I told you about?" Peter asks.

"Couldn't decide," Roger answers.

"He never can," his wife adds dryly.

"Your tits're showin' don't ya know," Pete throws at Elana.

"A judge in Guelph found it perfectly acceptable to bare breasts in public," Elana throws back.

"If you're built like a shit brickhouse," Pete says, his eyes fixed on her.

"Chicken *casserole?*" Elana drips disdain at Carrie. "I'm surprised you didn't make it tuna with potato chip topping. Jello mould with canned fruit. Canned peach halves in slimy liquid. Fifties food," she tells David.

"I wouldn't remember," Carrie answers.

"Maybe we should sing something," David says softly.

"Something from *Oklahoma*?" Roger asks.

"It's not what other people think about grey, it's the way *I* feel," Jan persists. "You should try a colouring," looking at the top of my head. "It would do wonders."

"How long you gonna sit there before you cover yourself up, for Chrissake, Elana?" Pete asks.

"It was fortuitous I wore underpants tonight," she remarks.

"Give her your jacket, Roger," Pete demands.

"Look Peter, if Sam were here he'd..." Elana begins.

"Sam was an asshole," says Pete.

"Peter!" Carrie cries, "That's enough, you've had too much to drink. Let me get you something to put on, Elana."

"Men aren't what they used to be," Elana says.

"Get her your purple, sweetheart," Roger says to his wife.

"I don't look good in purple," from Elana.

David's singing quietly, "*Oh what a beautiful morning...*"

"I met this guy at the university, this little short guy with a paunch and..." Jan begins telling me.

"Watch it, Jan, (nodding in my direction), she's takin' all this down in her head. You'll find yourself in a story," Peter tells her. "She'll snatch your words and prick your brain and make up her own ending."

"The Pink Panther, always sniffing around the rim of conversation," Jan agrees.

"Social Intercourse," Roger, smiling, picks up on Jan.

"*What about the beard, Roger?*" Pete asks.

"Here, try this," Carrie hands Elana a hostess gown she's brought down from her bedroom, "It suits you."

"Brown suits me?" Elana, offended.

"It goes with your hair," Jan smiles.

"The roots," Peter mumbles.

Elana's dropped crumbs on the crest of her right breast. Pete's eyes are glued to it.

"Try getting your black and white, Carrie," Roger instructs his wife.

"This guy with the paunch...," Jan says, turning back to me. "He had these long strands brushed over his bald top, trying to cover up I don't know what, he wasn't fooling anyone." She stops. "Oh for God's sake, Elana, take the fucking dress and be done with it!"

"Probably the same idiot bald guy my wife ran off with," from Peter. "What the hell does she see in the twerp? I dunno, twenty years and two kids..."

"It does make you feel like shit," Jan commiserates. Her eyes do a quick survey of Pete, up down, taking him all in. He's pushing forty-eight, a gentle pot straining against his red cable knit, still, attractive in a cigarette-dangling, trenchcoat, sort of way.

"What about *Pack up your troubles in your old kit bag and smile, smile, smile*? Roger asks David.

"David's too young for that one," Carrie tells her husband.

"What about the beard, Rog? What about your stupid fucking beard?" Pete demands.

"What about it?" Roger answers. "What about rain, what about the stock market, what about grey? Why does it bother you so much? What about *doing* it?"

"What about my ass!" Peter explodes. "This whole world is nuts! What do you see in this guy, Carrie?"

Carrie looks warmly over at Roger and smiles. "Oh, he has his appeal," she answers. He smiles back.

"What about it? Nothing, no reason. Variety, asymmetry, shock value. Duality of Life. Questions without answers. Mid-life rebellion," Roger, to Pete.

None of us answer.

The storm takes up the earth, rips open the sky, waves slam against boulders; thunder, lightning, slashing rain, whooshing wind, *I'll huff and I'll puff till I blow your house in*; windows quake and clatter; something outside has been blown over, falls onto the porch or against a rock, a crashing bouncing metal sound. The candle flickers; David's loops, Rog's gold chain, Elana's Peretti heart, glisten. She's in the black and white print, finishing desert (Apple-Brown Betty), covertly watching Carrie watch Roger. Jan's sipping wine, tucks her hair behind one ear, pretending to be unaware of Peter sizing her up. David's singing to himself, *There's a Brown Girl in the Ring, Tra-lalalala*. Carrie keeps a level gaze on her husband.

"What about it?" Roger, no longer laughing, repeats; raises serious eyes to meet ours, very quietly offers his words up to the elements: "Aspects of nature unresolved?"

Dear Doctor

FROM THE DESK OF ROSE ENFELD

Dear Dr. Thompson:

My hand trembles on the receiver. Silently I rehearse. No longer can I avoid the protection of those dedicated to my well-being! Your receptionist, Joy (so *earnestly* joyless!), your crisp nurse, Elizabeth (a treasure! So *few* crisp nurses left!).... Yourself. You see, Doctor, this is big stuff! We are talking possibly Life and Death! We are talking *My* Body, *My* Breasts! My *Tits*!

I'm driven to this screaming vulgarity, desperate to break through this childish fear, this mess of inadequacies that grip at the thought of your level gaze, those milky blue eyes, listening (your eyes *do* listen), your slow controlled medical explanations, *sotto voce,* sotto *sotto* voce, patient, acknowledging my intelligence (layman's though it is — lay*woman's*, really). Oh! The heavy seriousness of your *caring*! Awesome. Respect demanded, and given. I grope for words, stammer.

With phoney joviality I try winning over Joy with intimacies, "How've you been? Busy?"

"Hold the line, please," she responds in her flat voice.

And Elizabeth. Crisp. "I don't want to bother Dr. Thompson," I begin, "It's just a minor thing. Maybe *you* can answer my question...." I hate myself. A woman of the nineties and still a browner. Sucky.

"*Doctor* will have to speak to you," she crisps (They all say *Doctor*, generic noun, like *Father* as in Holy).

This is it: what I've been unable to spit out over the telephone even with written notes in front of me, after rehearsing again and again exactly what I want to say, each sentence word for word. Can't take chances here. No stumbling, no hint of uncertainty. Alas, I resort to communication by computer.

Do you remember, Doctor (I think it only right I use a capital, although I'm told none is necessary), do you remember a mammogram I had taken back in February? The one you agreed to schedule after I thought I felt a lump? You were out of the office when I came in, but your associate, Dr. Hildebrand gave it a feel. No need to get excited. The radiologist's report was quite unexceptional. *You* had faith throughout the entire six weeks the x-ray department was searching for the lost film, and you turned out to be correct. Fibroid adenoma. Common. It's nothing, you said. It didn't help, of course, when my neighbour found a shadow on her mammogram proved to be "something," thereby proving her Doctor wrong (so much for the old Yiddish expression, "something is better than nothing"). Lucky for her, her Doctor sent her to a breast specialist as a courtesy, who aspirated the nothing, as a courtesy (my friend's a Doctor's wife), only to find a something. Oops! Surprise! I controlled my impulse to ask for the same courtesy and pushed all doubts aside.

Until the following November. I worked up enough courage to once more let my fingers do the walking, firmly around the perimeter of the right breast, around and around in smaller and smaller circles working toward the nipple, straining, listening more than feeling it seemed. Everything copacetic here. Then the left. Around and around again. Objective, dispassionate fingers, flat, making little circular motions like rubbing out a stain. There it is again. That lump. Bigger? I test again. Not so dispassionate this time, the fingers more earnest, listening more intensely. I called your office with no hesitation. Ode to Joy.

You were out of the office (again) when I came in, but a Resident examined me. I'm embarrassed to admit a crisis of faith when she appeared younger than my own daughter, a frightening thought if you knew my daughter. And there was that nagging voice, my mother's, coming from the centre of my being, heard, I imagined, clearly throughout your office, "*A WOMAN DOCTOR?*" I examined her face, Dr. Pathmanathan's, Dr. Shahbandu Kashvi Pathmanathan. Oh God! That too! Would she hear my mother's voice about that too? Would it sound like *my* voice? *Was* it mine? But Dr. Pathmanathan apparently heard nothing. "Is this the place?" she asked, feeling. Listening.

It wasn't, actually. I redirected her from the right breast to the left. She checked my file once more as if believing *it* the more reliable, but her puzzled expression indicated some discrepancy. "It does say *right* here," she said.

"No, I assure you it's *left*," I answered.

She looked down at the file again. "It *does* say right," she repeated. "Just another moment," she said as she riffled through the papers. "Ah, yes, the radiologist's report indicates *left*," she said, relieved, and flipped the papers back again. "Dr. Thompson made a slight error in transcribing. But it does say *right*, you see," she finished, showing me the report.

I nodded and said comforting things. "But," I said, "Could someone please circle the spot on the correct breast with a marker should I need to have ... you know, if I'm under anaesthesia and not available?"

"Not to worry," Dr. Pathmanathan assured me and continued with her probing.

"Mm. No, no change." She held up a small, white ruler. "Still only one cm. Really, it's nothing. I'd see Dr. Thompson and keep a check on it. Have another mammogram in a year," she smiled.

I nodded in agreement, and determined to have one within two months. Not that I looked forward to the indignity of having my breasts laid on a platter then flattened between plastic plates like a sandwich. It's a contorted way to get one's picture taken and a far cry from the titillating appeal of an eight-by-ten glossy.

I dressed but felt older than when I came in. Dr. Pathmanathan was such a quietly confident young woman. A Doctor! My relationship with her was clearly not the same as that with my daughter.

Which brings us to the present. Not wishing to be a pest — you recall your conviction that mammograms be given every *two* years, your concern being the costs to the system? — I phoned Women's College Hospital. They received me warmly, but the catch was I'd need a referral from you. Oh, no! Joy again, and Ms. Crisp, and the unbearable *sotto voce*. What's the worst-case response? I asked myself. Having steeled myself for that, I was unprepared for what followed. "Don't you *like* us here?" Joy asked. So plaintive! Cast now as underdog, wounded game, she became at once worthy of my sympathy.

I couldn't leave her disabled so, impotent, exposed. "Don't *like* you! What has this to do with *like*?" I asked Joy and hastened to give my reasons for deserting the institution that had paternalistically, altruistically, watched over me, and for which I'd had so little appreciation. Ingrate! I chided myself. "*DOCTOR* will return your call," Joy said. Her normally cool flat voice edged with annoyance sounded weak, crushed. This was much worse than anything I anticipated. Couldn't she have been simply hateful?

You did return my call, Dr. Thompson. You, too, asked, "Don't you like us?" Again I hastened to reassure, explain that I wanted a second opinion and a mammogram within less time than you were willing to schedule. But this love thing ... it motivates us all, doesn't it, Doctor? It strikes me that without the manifest bestowal of love from patients (the public), the medical profession must seek the only symbolic redress possible. Money. Finally I understand the CMA's insistence on control over payment. It's to do with LOVE! I wonder that wasn't apparent before. It's so obvious now! And explains an incident that happened to me last year with Doctor Epstein. Dr. Epstein, the gynecologist? I went to him as follow-up to my hysterectomy (more accurately *her*terectomy, for if we're to believe hyster, meaning hysteria, refers to women, why not *her*teria? And *her*terectomy?) I could have forgiven being kept waiting while he delivered a baby, but when he returned to the office he announced, checking his watch, "Fifteen minutes! Twenty, tops, including time to get up to O.R. and back." Oh, he was proud. Rightly, I thought. So efficient!

But then I asked, "Did the baby come fully equipped? Was it a boy or girl?" I remember he was caught up short and said, "I don't know! I forgot to look!" I worried for a moment about the baby's parts, but Epstein seemed undisturbed.

However, that's not what I set out to tell you, Dr. Thompson. What followed will be relevant, I think. To be fair I should mention that two hours after the delivery, still waiting, flipping through *Redbook, Cosmopolitan* and *Reader's Digest,* watching pregnant women come and go, I was already out of sorts when the nurse led me into the examining room.

Dr. Epstein must have picked up my mood when he entered because he threw me a sidelong glance and asked sheepishly, "You're annoyed with me? I kept you waiting?"

"Well, I'm not too pleased," I found voice to say, too mildly, muttered something about my time being valuable and noted that no self-respecting man would have waited that long.

"No, but there aren't any pregnant men I know of," he laughed. "How's the bleeding been?"

I looked at him blankly. "Bleeding?"

"Mm. How're the periods? Still taking Premarin and Provera?"

I explained to him he'd operated on me six months ago. He opened my file. "So, how do you feel?" He brightened, remembering. "I did a great job, I must say. Hardly a scar at all! A little bikini tuck." He looked as pleased as when he'd announced the baby-person's birth so I hadn't the heart to complain too much, but I had to tell him how depressed I was, perhaps it was hormonal, shock to the system. I was never comfortable about the ovaries coming out even though he'd assured me I wouldn't be needing them much longer, four-five years, maybe. "*Vei, vei,*" he commiserated and gave me that sidelong glance again. His eyes grew dark and serious, contemplative; he leaned forward and placed his hand gently on my knee. "Sometimes ... at this time in a woman's life, a man begins to behave ... strangely. Brings little presents maybe." When he saw the puzzled expression on my face, Dr. Thompson, he tried again. "Some men can't do what they used to. It doesn't mean they don't love their wives anymore ... or any less."

"Are you saying my husband can't get it up!" I exclaimed. Epstein pulled back.

On reflection, I have to admire his restraint, the delicate way he came at a touchy problem. Or what he thought was the problem. And why not? After all, Dr. Thompson, a woman's interests, talents, and emotions are so tied to husband and children (aren't they?), her bonding to those around her so deep, so strong, it's only appropriate (medically speaking) to see her depression in light of those relationships, the most effectual being that of her husband as lover. Acknowledging that to allow such melancholy to persist would have a profound impact on the family, Epstein had no choice but to explore the performance aspect. He might have hit it head on in the blunt manner of men, asking for instance, "Has there been any change in your sexual relationship with your husband?" but obviously thinking that too direct and insensitive, chose instead the subtler, more oblique approach of women. Roundabout. Less threatening. The sophistication of Epstein's technique wasn't clear to me until later; unhappily, I hadn't fully appreciated him.

But you see, don't you, Dr. Thompson, how much importance the medical profession attaches to love? That's not all, however. What happened next will prove what I mean. Epstein didn't respond to my *can't get it up*! but said, "We'll have a look." (The Royal "We.") "But first read this. If you have any questions, ask. Sign at the bottom and I'll call my nurse in to witness it."

I glanced quickly through the *Open Letter to Our Faithful Patients from Drs. Epstein and McLeod, Associates.* "But this says I agree these overage fees are legal," I protested. "Wasn't this issue settled by the Doctors' strike?"

He explained that the amounts paid by the Government Health Insurance were not nearly enough to cover costs. "Do you want Doctors forced to run to the *United States*?" he asked and handed me his pen. "Well, you don't have to sign, no problem," withdrawing it, "We'll just put this aside," and took the paper from me.

"No, you don't understand," I stopped him. I hated myself for the tremor in my voice, but my sense of social outrage had been pricked and I plunged forward. "I agree with the Government!" He was startled, seemingly unprepared for this idea. "I resent being invaded with your politics — with *this!*" I picked up the paper and shook it in front of him, "It's tough enough being invaded, having to surrender to your probing and pushing and poking around inside my body so please leave my head alone."

Epstein did whatever is meant by "sputter and fume." Clearly he was shaken. "Why aren't you complaining about how the Government is treating *your* Doctor?"

"You still don't get it," I answered. "I don't agree with you." Epstein exploded. "This must mean you don't love me!"

YOU DON'T *LOVE* ME! There it is, Dr. Thompson. The Love thing. Not the Money thing, as I'd thought. Love. Everybody sings about it. Remember the Beatles, Dr. Thompson, *All You Need Is Love?* Or writes about it, philosophizes on it, Plato, Dante, Leo Bascaglia, and now I see it's the motivating force behind modern medicine, more specifically, behind the Canadian Medical Association. I wouldn't have believed it, but here was proof in the person of my GYN speaking for multitudes of misunderstood maligned doctors! Never had I understood the power I had to hurt. I thought again of the hundreds of file folders packed together tight as cattle in a slaughterhouse, with all that penned-up power to gore the heart of Dr. Epstein!

I was (in a manner of speaking) caught on the horns of a dilemma. Touched by Epstein's need for love, I was at the same time scornful of it. Would he have expected the same devotion from my husband? I think not, Dr. Thompson. For instance, after I protested with, "Love You! Good heavens! I most certainly do not. What does love have to do with our relationship?"

Epstein then asked in a demanding way, "What does your husband do?"

Why would Epstein want to know about him? What was I, chopped liver? "What does it matter?" I asked. Perhaps I was missing something.

"I *want* to know," he insisted.

There was a subtext (there always is), and I knew what it was. So I played to it. "He's a public servant, a Paleontologist for the ROM, paid a set wage, like teachers, university professors, social workers, and bureaucrats." Epstein's subtext hadn't taken that possibility into account. He'd prepared a counterargument for businessman, or lawyer; dentist. Now I ask you, Dr. Thompson, could you see *me* married to a *dentist*?

"There you have it!" Epstein exploded. He was feverish. He yanked at his hair so the strands brushed over his bald top flew wild, his eyes bugged out, large ears reddened, hunched fleshy shoulders leaned toward me and a poky fat finger shook in my face. "That's what they're trying to do. Make us the same as teachers and social workers. Control us. Take away our power." And then, Dr. Thompson, Epstein slumped as if by the very mentioning of taking away his power all his potency was sucked from him. His life force drained. He looked very sad, bewildered. Poor Epstein. Denied the essentials of existence: Love and Power. You see how mistaken I'd been about *everything*! I'd simplistically put the medical fraternity's beef down to the money thing.

He went on. "We're headed for Socialism!" he cried, shaking his head, propping it up with his hand. Could he have been a clairvoyant, predicting as none of us could at that time the New Democrats' sweep of Ontario? "A Socialist country, that's what!" he threw at me.

"Controlled greed," I threw back. I'd lost all my natural reserve, all tendency to cringe at seeing another embarrassed. The tourniquet had been removed, my thoughts no longer wrapped by the fear and mess of inadequacies I struggled to overcome when confronted with your unruffled person, Dr. Thompson, as I've explained earlier. Epstein, with his *lantzman's* familiarity, his Yiddishkite invitation to debate, his *vei, vei-ing,* had challenged my social scruples, thereby igniting my anger, my passion, released (unwittingly) that brazen, outspoken, magnificent woman you, with all your measured caring and deference, were unable to free. That confident assertive woman I always knew was there, latently, potentially powerful like the genie in the bottle.

Oh, and the genie *was* out! It was when Epstein cried that he'd entered a profession promising status, money and power (I think he forgot the Love part), and after years of having enjoyed those gifts — hard-earned and well deserved he pointed out — all of Doctordom was about to be stripped, reduced to salaried employees no better than social workers, it was then I let him have it. "Move over, Doctor. You and your Associate, Dr. McLeod. Speed off on your boat docked at Port Hope, with your coiffed wife (chemical-blonde) who does good works on the Women's Symphony Committee and National Ballet Board, your Urologist and Proctologist sons, off to your Florida condo. Move over, make room for the younger ones."

And then he surrendered, or appeared to. Placing the *Open*

Letter in his out basket, he sighed, "Fine. We'll put this aside" (the royal We again. It was big of him, he had no hard feelings) and began to write on a memo pad, "...and just deal with each service as it comes up.... Let's see, thirty-five for each prescription renewal, thirty-five for..."

At that moment I was glorious, Dr. Thompson. I stood up, tall, regal, and in my most controlled voice said, "I think it best I leave. I wouldn't feel comfortable with your palm in my interior. No gratuitous gropes!" And I left him. For good. Jilted. He asked for love and what did he get? Nothing! *Bubkas*! How did I feel Dr. Thompson? Great! Like discovering how it feels to be part of an ethnic majority. Powerful!

I tried to recall that feeling when once again faced with the Love question, first from Joy, then you, Dr. Thompson. But there it was, your level blue eyes and *sotto voce*, the exterior calm, the assumed, awesome Word of The Healer. I assured you at the time of the high regard, if not love, I felt for you, and you agreed to schedule the mammogram, put aside your concerns over cost to the system. Our resolve, however, is constantly being tested. No more than a day after you and I settled our differences I read in the *Toronto Star* a letter to Ann Landers from a woman recounting how a something was mistaken for a nothing, the result of which led to parting with a uniquely feminine portion of her upper body. Her Doctor hadn't considered a biopsy necessary. Pity. He didn't think she had a problem.

My problem, Dr. Thompson, became the need to advance once more through the front lines, Mses. Joyless and Crisp, reach the Top Gun (you), to present as ammunition a letter printed in an Advice-to-the-Lovelorn column. With my hand trembling on the receiver, I struggled with the consequences of letting the whole matter drop. Whose life was it anyway? Whose body? Whose Love and who was deserving of its bestowal? The answers were clear. What was it precisely I wanted? "I WANT...," I heard myself say aloud, practicing,

"I want to see a Breast Man, uh ... Person." I sounded as if I were ordering chicken parts from a butcher. It was no different, I reasoned, from asking to see a rectal specialist for hemorrhoids. A *tushy* Doctor. We are all in the end (no pun intended) pieces of meat in a chorus line. *Tits and Ass!* But my wit would be lost. Joy would say flatly, "Hold the line, please," and Elizabeth, "You want a referral? Ultrasound? Biopsy? I'll have *Doctor* call you back," and I would wait for your call all the while predicting your counterarguments, jotting down my responses, rehearsing.

No! No! Screw It! I'll write.

Patiently,

Rose Enfeld

Shayndeleh

SAME EVERY DAY SINCE MOVING IN, Jeanne gazes into the large fish tank in the Dubin House library, following streaks of calico and gold, orange, blue and black, darting back and forth under the surface of the water. Her eyes track the canary yellows with black stripes and translucent tails and finally settle on the silver-white goldfish weaving in, out and around the archways and towers of a sand-coloured castle. Jeanne calls her Queenie, Queen of the castle. It's different from all the other fish in the tank; Jeanne likes that it's different and thinks it the prettiest. It has a startling, strawberry-red crown, puffy as if permed and given a bouffant styling. Jeanne knows she's on the outside looking in, yet she feels a bond with Queenie. Now and again, it swims over to the glass to stare back at her, then with a flutter of its gauzy fins and tail, sweeps around and returns to its home.

That's when Jeanne says what she says about fish and their worries, a remark that Tzippi probably doesn't appreciate, but Jeanne doesn't care. Tzippi has spent the last hour talking; listening, too, but she doesn't *hear* a damn thing, never does. No one does. Course, the whole time, Tzippi keeps sounding like a know-it-all. Jeanne remembers how the afternoon began, remembers herself saying, "Don't grow old."

"The alternative isn't so good," from Tzippi. "You're still the same person as when you were young."

Jeanne gazes directly at Tzippi, seated beside her, trying to fathom the meaning of her words, then silently looks down at her hands and strokes one with the fingertips of the other. "*'I dree-am of Jeannie with the light bro-own hair,'*" Tzippi sings softly.

Jeanne nods, recalling how everyone used to say the song was written just for her. She turns her face to the sun coursing through the windows of Dubin House Geriatric. She likes that name, Jeannie, but people mostly call her Jenny — which she hates — or sometimes *Shayndeleh* — the pretty one. She knows she's pretty, she can *see*, can't she? Pictures of when she was young are proof — a princess, everyone said, her skin so unblemished and blushing, her eyes so clear; green, sometimes blue, like ice water. Her hair's white now, and the nurses tell her it's beautiful. Striking, is what they say, and ask, who does the colour? which amuses her no end.

She was slender too. Her father, "Pops" — a tailor in the *shmatteh* business — sewed clothes for her that looked like she came from money. Her eyes spark with humour just re-membering, but that quickly fades. She's *fat*, short and fat, four foot, eleven inches, and size fourteen, she berates herself, and when she puts her down jacket on to go out — when ... *if* ... her sister thinks to come for her — she feels like a bloated lump in a wheelchair.

Unseeing, she peers out at the grassy courtyard. Actually, she's staring further on, at the low-rise apartment building a short distance beyond.

"The alternative is not to be around at all," Tzippi says.

Jeanne shakes her head side-to-side. She doesn't understand what's so difficult for people to get.

"That's right, isn't it?" Tzippi tries.

What does *Tzippi* know? Jeanne thinks. "You're young. You shouldn't talk, Tzippi, until you're wearin' *my* moccasins. It's one thing if you grow old inside, but what about when you're old *outside*?"

She thinks *that* may have gotten to Tzippi.

"Do you recognize that building over there?" Tzippi asks, ignoring her question. She points to the low-rise with its defining turquoise balconies. "It's where you lived before you moved in here, remember?"

"No."

"You lived there when Maury was alive…? Tzippi, her voice inflecting upward as if asking for agreement, a habit that never fails to irritate Jeanne. Remember when all your brothers and sisters and all the kids used to crowd into your tiny apartment and laughed and talked so loud…?"

"No, I don't remember nothin', " I said.

"Your brother Lou — Lou and Etta — lived down the hall…? And Maxine — your sister Maxine and Sam — on the floor below…? Everybody in and out; then Maury died and…"

Jeanne nods her head slowly.

"Remember how we'd walk into the building and meet two or three Gersteins hanging about the lobby, standing around that fountain with the fake palm tree? Why, we even called the whole *building* Gerstein Towers!" Tzippi laughs.

Jeanne turns a blank stare to her niece, thinking how she used to have such nice dark hair, the colour of chestnuts. She used to be attractive and dress nice. Then she married one a the orthodox and now she's kosher an' nuts. What Jeanne considers *over*-Jewish. Calls herself Tzipporah instead of Sarah and wears dresses like for an old lady. She's still young, forty-somethin'!

"Okay then, let's talk about *now*," Tzippi tries.

Jeanne thinks Tzippi must be stupid. There *is* no now.

She casts her eye around the area looking out onto the courtyard. Tzippi's gaze follows. A few residents are outside chatting, some seated on benches, some standing, supported by walkers; inside, most slump down in wheelchairs, dozing, their chins to their chests, their bodies listless and overweight from too many starchy foods and desserts. Grey-heads, all; women. The few men able enough to stand on their own are each surrounded by two or three equally able, unmistakably admiring women.

"Do *you* see anything to talk about?" Jeanne puts to her niece.

"Well, there must be shopping trips. Or Bingo," Tzippi says, turning back to her, her voice upbeat. "Don't you play Bingo? Gin Rummy? *You* like cards. I know *something's* going on."

"With those crazy people? Why am *I* here? My mind is good. I *told* them." Confusion registers across her face, in her eyes. She'll leave this place. She can do it. She doesn't need anybody's help, not her son Arnie's, not Tzippi's, and not her brother Lou's. The fingers of one hand tight together, she draws tiny circling motions on her thigh with her fingertips.

"I'm so angry!" she exclaims abruptly. "I'm ... just a minute, I'll tell you..." she drifts off, sifting through a catalogue of hurts. What was it that had so infuriated? The incident, gone; it doesn't matter, the *feeling* still burns. Her eyes flash and her voice tremors with emotional recall. "*Yesterday* ... yesterday I..."

She knows this feeling of anger; it's familiar, intimate and warm; the sensation sits in her bones, her chest and shoulders, tingles at the bridge of her nose and back of her neck, pushes behind her eyes. The anger charges forward, on automatic, if only she could find the memory.

Her gaze drifts to a place beyond Tzippi's shoulder. "Oh, *this* one's crazy," she mutters as a thin, neatly dressed woman in culottes and white runners comes up and stands beside Tzippi.

"Excuse me, Mister," the woman says — though no Misters are there — "Will you show me how to do this?" She holds out a bright yellow piece of knitted yarn with wide green trim, suspended from crocheting needles. "It's a hat," touching her fingers to salt and pepper hair.

"Sorry," Tzippi answers.

"Do you want me to show you?" the woman offers. "There, you see?" she says, completing several stitches, then stops. "Will you help me?" she asks, a puzzled expression on her face.

"Jenny knows how. Show her, Jen."

Jeanne winces, but takes the crocheting in her hand, finishes the row. "There," giving it back to the woman.

"I can't. Will you show me?" Worried, dark eyes implore.

Overhearing, a nurse strolls over, grasps her by the arm. "Come, Anna, let's leave these nice women alone."

"Will you show me?"

"Anna!" the nurse says sharply, and firmly begins edging her away. "Will we see you for Bingo tonight, Jeanne?" she calls back over her shoulder.

She shakes her head no.

"For Mah Jong tomorrow then?"

Jeanne looks away. Gradually, her focus shifts to a plastic toiletries holder on her lap. With a slight tremor, her fingers pull at its zipper. She peers inside, sifts through the contents, eventually withdraws a small silver compact, opens it and, fumbling with the catch, examines herself critically in its mirror: she takes the powder puff, pats her chin, nose and cheeks, and replaces the puff. Now she knows exactly what she's after. She retrieves a gold lipstick tube. Drawing her upper lip tight to her teeth, with deliberate movements, she strokes the rouge onto it — right, centre, left — sweeps the lipstick across the lower, presses the lips together, rechecks herself in the mirror. Satisfied, she closes the compact and puts it back.

"Mr. Lieberman told me at breakfast I look pretty," she says, brightening.

"And so you do," Tzippi answers.

"But they didn't let me have any breakfast," Jeanne says, her eyes suddenly teary, her expression turned childlike. "I didn't eat *anything*. A bit of cereal, a little coffee … nothin'."

"I know what. Why don't I do your nails? You have a file and some polish in your bag?" Tzippi asks. Taking the plastic holder from her, Tzippi finds both and begins filing the nails of her aunt's right hand. "Such fine nails; so well-shaped. There! Now let's have your other hand."

Jeanne inspects Tzippi's work and nods approval. She likes having her nails done, likes Tzippi's full attention. She doesn't get it from her son or daughter. They live far away. They *say* they come to see her, but they don't; *say* they were just here, but they weren't; she doesn't remember any such thing. She leans in to watch Tzippi brush polish onto her fingernails. It's a nice colour. Delicate pink, like Jeanne's blush. When Tzippi has finished polishing, Jeanne holds both hands up for view.

"That's better. A lot better than the lousy job the young kid in *this* place does. Even better than the *shvartze* at Penny's used to. I'm tellin' you, I only wish the girl here'd get *blacker!*" Jeanne laughs.

"You look *so* relaxed and lovely when you smile, Shayndeleh," Tzippi says, capping the polish, putting it and the file back in the case; ignoring the Yiddish slur.

Jeanne *knows* she was being funny, and her eyes still laugh at the absurdity of what she said. She throws a sideways glance at her niece, hoping for a smile at least — or a rise. Well, what would you expect? All of a sudden Tzippi's so over-*correct*, ever since she got over-Jewish. All of a sudden she's got a "responsibility to fix the world," uses Hebrew words that sound to Jeanne like *tickin'* along. Personally, she thinks Tzippi's tryin' to show off. Why not Yiddish, something Jeanne could understand? No, Tzipp*orah* (and why not *Sarah*?) has got to be smarter — more good — than the rest of us. In Jeanne's opinion, she just got more humourless.

As far as looking "lovely" when she smiles, people tell her that all the time, so Tzippi's just bein' ... how do you say it? ... *patronizing*. Does she think she's a child?

"I need to go upstairs and get washed up now, company's coming."

"Who?"

"Company. I need to get dressed. Get the box of candy, Rachel, you know, where I always keep it, in the china closet."

"Jeanne, I'm Tzippi, and..."

"I don't want to be late. Where's Maury?"

"He's ... downstairs," Tzippi lies.

"He's never around when I need him. The table needs to be set and I want him to check the roast. I need to go get dressed."

"You're thinking about a long time ago, the house on Raritan, remember? Where you lived before moving into that building — see, there? With the turquoise balconies...?" pointing in its direction. "That's when Maury worked at the Towers Theatre. When Maxine and Sam lived down the street from you, and Lou and Etta at the other end. Jeanne settles a level look on Tzippi, but seems mildly puzzled, as if she'd slipped off somewhere and is surprised to find herself here, in this place. Yeah, she thinks. Maury brought back bagel and whitefish from Fagie's Deli on Sunday mornings, and she'd make coffee and Maxine and Sam and their kids would drop in, an' maybe some of the others. Everybody in and out.

"You raised your children in that house," Tzippi persists. "Rachel was taking dance and cello, and Arnie..."

"Yeah, a lot happening. Maury and I..." Her brow creases and she lapses into quiet, trying to follow the thought; once again her attention drifts to the toiletries holder on her lap, and once again quivering fingers struggle with the zipper. This time, she opens the holder, takes out an envelope and riffles through the papers inside. "I must take care of this. If I don't get to the bank the day these cheques come, it doesn't get done. If I had my car..."

"I think they're cancelled cheques, Jen."

"Yeah," she murmurs, putting the envelope back in the case, and continues searching; finally settles on an address book. Still delicate, she thinks, seeing her hands leaf through it — she always had nice hands, the nails well groomed, like now. She feels Tzippi watching her every move. Several loose papers with notes scrawled on them wedge between the pages. Jeanne reads one, forming the words with her lips; shakes her head side-to-side, trying to fathom its message, when it was written.

"I don't need them," she says after examining each, then hands the papers to Tzippi and returns to flipping through the book. "Aaron Aronowitz, Helen and Marty Taub, Sylvia Ratner, Helen Patterson...." She doesn't see those people anymore. Why don't they call? Did they die?

Seconds go by as she continues turning the pages, reading the lists.

Where did it all go, and how did this happen? Did the years shrink down to a plastic "purse" housing scraps from her life? Names in an old address book?

"What I'm looking for isn't here," she says at last and puts it back into the case.

"Mm. You'll find it another time, don't worry," Tzippi comforts. "Aunt Jenny, I'm going to have to get going...."

"Where're you runnin' off to?" Jeanne asks, anxiety springing to her eyes as she sees Tzippi check her watch. She's always runnin' off. So're Jeanne's daughter Rachel and son Arnie. Sure, Arnie stops in — on his way to New York. Always runnin' — Jeanne's sisters and brothers too.

"I can stay a few more minutes, but I'm afraid I'll have to be on my way. I'll be back," she reassures. "Besides, it's almost time for your dinner. Come, I'll walk with you to your room," reaching for her jacket and handbag.

"They have lousy food here," Jeanne complains, for the umpteenth time, she thinks, but it does no good, nobody listens. She allows Tzippi to help her out of her seat and to her walker, then hangs the straps of the plastic case around the handle and takes tentative steps forward. They make their way to the lobby, stopping to gaze into a large tank set on a pedestal in the library. Silent for the longest time, Jeanne stares at the fish, orange and black and silver, her mind slipping back to how Tzippi tried to convince her she was still the same person as when she was young. What does *she* know? Pretending there was something going on here that was worth a life, worth talking about.

Jeanne keeps her attention on the fish. Back and forth they swim, as if going somewhere, their gauzy tails fanning out, gently disturbing the clear water. They slalom in and around leafy plants swaying gently with the flow, nuzzle cobalt blue and emerald rocks at the bottom of the tank and chase after champagne bubbles burbling to the top. Jeanne's gaze follows the silver-white one with the strawberry-red crown as it floats in and out and around the castle, as Shayndeleh has seen her do so many times she can't count; then along its parapet, around its turrets, through its doorway again, again and again. She can't take her eyes off it. Every so often it swims over to the glass, hovers there, its dark eyes staring back at Jeanne, its mouth making tiny puck-puck movements, as if asking what's she's doing on the outside, looking in; then sweeps around and goes back to surveying its castle.

"Beautiful, aren't they?" Tzippi offers. "It's all so calm and peaceful, don't you think, Aunt Jenny?"

Seconds of silence go by like minutes, weighted with a lifetime of pleasures made bittersweet with present sorrows.

"Aunt Jenny?"

"Yeah," she murmurs at last. "Yeah, the fish have no worries. Nobody pushed *them* outa *their* home."

She allows that thought to suspend in air. See what Tzippi has to say about *that* one. Finally Tzippi breaks the stillness.

"I must leave now. I'll come visit again, I promise."

Pulling her glance away from the tank, Jeanne grasps tightly onto the handlebar of her walker and settles a flat emotionless look onto her niece. Oh, she's angry, but the lingering image of the silver-white fish with the strawberry-red crown, the way she asserted her claim to her castle, stayed close, a homeowner protecting her property — stared down Jeanne, like she was an intruder — the whole powerful impression, has diffused the anger, now part resentment, part resolve, part self-pity; hope, sadness and despair, wistfulness. Fantasy.

She'll leave this place. This isn't the first time she's thought about it; it's been on her mind the whole time Tzippi's been here, talking nonsense. Though she did do her nails good, and she *is* kind, that much Jeanne will grant. But now she's resolved to quit this Home that will never be home. All she'll need will be a small bag with a nightgown, underwear, a few tops and a couple pair of slacks, her plastic holder with some toiletries, medicines, tweezers, her small mirror and compact, lipstick, comb and her address book. She thinks she'll take her cane and leave the walker behind, like useless baggage. She'll take off right after breakfast and, once outside, board the van to … she's not sure. But she'll get herself to the station and buy a one-way ticket.

Next time Tzippi comes to visit — or Rachel or Arnie, or Shayndeleh's sisters or brothers — she won't be here. She'll be on a bus to Somewhere.

She doesn't know where. She'll just ride.

Tikkun-olam: A Hebrew phrase meaning "repairing, or perfecting, the world." In Judaism, performing mitzvoth (good deeds), is a requirement, to help make the world a better place.

The Day of the Gorgon

ONE OVERCAST DAY AFTER FIERCE STORMS, while walking along the beach in Southern California, suddenly sensing danger, Marek grasped Katya's arm. "What is it Marek? What is it?" she cried.

On that day he was with his wife Katherine collecting stones by the sea, as was his habit. Most often he found them on the shores of Lake Simcoe where he and Katherine live, away from the city he fears, seeing everywhere hooligans in alleyways and under streetlamps; brown shirts overrunning night. Here, by the lake, away from the wail of sirens, shouts, and shrill laughter, he writes fiction, a labour of most of his 74 years, searching to make sense of non-sense. Ultimately words fail.

But this time, they were in San Diego for the worst of the winter months. He remembers the beach that day, sand and sea and sky tilting, seaweed at his feet shivering, shifting, rising and rolling. Remembers breaking into a cold sweat, how he passed his hand over his eyes, thinking, I am having one of my dizzy spells!

Night terrors.

*

He's enclosed in a small windowless space hot as an incinerator or a brick oven baking in desert sun, herded in, crushed from all sides, a stench like that of human waste or burning flesh so present and vile, he gags even as he sleeps; rumbling fills his

95

head and wailing and high-pitched cries and screams mingled with his own weak *help*! Try as he might his plea is strangled, and again and again he tries, each time straining louder but only a thin feeble whimper escapes.

No one answers. He's sick from heat and the smell and what seems like constant motion, and the rumbling. Suddenly, a deep voice commands, *"Bist du ein Jude?"*

Bist du ein Jude! ... He jolts awake, in a sweat, dizzy and terrified. Shadows loom, wiry lines slash walls. Several moments of white panic pass before he recognizes them as slats of venetian blinds Katherine has used as window cover, the room's light not the focused glare of a spotlight, but the wash of the moon.

*

Slowly, the ticking of the clock at the foot of the stairs enters his consciousness and he lies awake listening for its chime through the long night into morning when day breaks and he's reassured once more the sun will rise. When Katherine, his Katya, is away at her sister's in Montreal, he is alone and the house is quiet. Younger than he, a handsome woman of confidence and energy, she bumps around the cottage filling it with the sound of her voice, "Ah! Of *course*! ... It's *extraooo*-rd'nary!" Running upstairs, long skirts flowing about her legs, she calls, "Marek? Monsieur Markeovitch!" and bounds into his room, her feet coming firmly down, splayed and flat-footed, the gait of ballerinas. The clock chimes three-thirty. No use lying here he thinks getting up, sleep will be no haven, reading no comfort, nor writing down his thoughts. Ach! These murderous thoughts he wishes to tear from his brain. He will make a list. Another habit, though some call it compulsion, like gathering stones from the beach. Once in his den, surrounded by his books, the familiar touch of warm wood under his hand, his nerves at last begin to settle. I can only tell you, he is fond of saying, I *love* it, this secure feeling.

Yes, his list, he'll make several: under A, those he can depend on absolutely; under B, most of the time; C, sometimes, *maybe*, but he'll shift them from list to list as he sees fit. Katherine of course is in the A column. Should she not be well, or here? Here at all, that is? One never knows.

Did he forget to say he has children? The question is, on which list does he place them? Surely not A. Rubbing his eyes, he stares at the silent phone. It's not rung since his wife called from her sister's two days ago. Ah! the wire twists! he observes, righting the receiver in its cradle. Finally, he writes his sons' names in the space under B; reflecting a moment, moves them to C. Then turns to friends. Friends by appointment ... *Lunch next Saturday, one o'clock?* He is too harsh; surely a few deserve to be under B ... Steinberg, Miller, Knellman. He writes in their names all the while doubting, his mind a mass of confusion. Lists imply efficiency, no? *Another time*, he thinks and passes his hand again over his eyes.

Later. He will finish the lists later, choose then.

His father made lists: Who Owes Money; goods received; credit extended; money borrowed. We needed coin to purchase freedom. Who can we count on? Yes, Who. Customer Gorczyn? Dr. Wolf? Neighbour Zielinski?

To his father everyone was an A. He made *one* such list, then another to replace the first, and another and another until it became clear his question was not reasonable, only one question mattered: *Bist du ein Jude?*

No, Marek will have *three* lists, for he is not so optimistic and will move names around, relocate them, so to speak. Of course all must be judged by just one criterion, who can be counted, who will come to his aid. Other lists have been far more discriminating, a matter of choosing, sorting, classifying: young, old, weak, strong, sick, disabled; ugly, *schone*, fat, stupid; useful ... whore. Then the relocating ... *ubersiedlung*: you to rot, You get shot, you starve, you die; you to work ... ARBEIT MACHT FREI!

Well, others are right, what good to dwell, to see so many ghosts? What drives him to, how should he say it ... take inventory? To make a long story short, the phone does not ring anymore. He tried to tell his own father once, *Be done with your lists! There is no one.* Finally, he was himself on a list, to make a long story short.

*

Marek leaves his list-making, and in dawn's half-light huddles before bookshelves in his den, studying the dictionary, thesaurus, hunting for words or expressions to relax more his English; help his writing sound more natural. If only he could write in Polish what he has to tell, if only others could understand *his* language. Well, he keeps hoping, *this day* or the next, or next, he'll *find the right words* to tell of these horrors, purge shadow places his eye folds in upon.

There are people who say Marek Wronski is obsessed with only one subject, that which terrorizes him. Dwells too much in the past, they say, it isn't healthy. Of course, they said these things even back when his books were being published. Write an autobiography and be done with it! they said. They understand little. Fiction distances him, allows him to tell the truth.

You see, he *must* dwell...

Arranging words, compiling names, assembling stones....

*

Words miscarry memory; lists lie, unreliable. And so, he abandons these efforts, and drawn by the full light of morning, cloudless blue sky, and shimmering lake, goes out to his work shed by the water's edge and turns his energy to making small sculptures from stones he'd gathered that frightening day by the sea.

A twig for an arm, piece of branch a leg, acorn feet; polished pebble a nose, berries for eyes; birds' feathers, fungi, dried leaves and flowers, outlandish hat! Strong glue, shellac, a few touches of red paint. "I can only tell you," he confides to Katherine, "this gives me such pleasure! I feel ... I don't know, how can I put it? ... Lighter!" She says she sees how his eyes brighten, his ruddy cheeks flush as if from too much wine. He thinks he looks like a slight bird with his sharp bones and small beaked nose, an old, straight-backed tipsy bird, foolish as his creations.

Who would guess Marek Wronski possesses such whimsy! Certainly Katherine and her friends don't understand his humour. They are Canadian, brought up on U.S. culture: cowboys and Indians, and what she calls "sitcoms" and "slapstick." "Tell me, Katharina," addressing her as he would a Russian princess, "what do these shows stand for? What is their purpose?"

"Why, entertainment!" she cries, and clasping her hands to her heart, croons, "*Stop! In the name of love* ... The sixties! *The Supremes*, Marek!" and laughs at him for not getting it. What planet has he been on?

Now, on this cloudless morning, in his workshop by the water's edge, he contemplates his crafted bit of fancy and chuckling begs her examine it. What to use for a *shlong*? This closed-up-tight pine cone, shameful shy little one, tinier than his baby fingernail? This medium one, opened wide like the kiss of flower petals? Or this long, grandiose holder of seed? Only the wistful little one folded into itself seems right. Still, Marek thinks, examining it, it *does* have potential, even if all seems barren.

"This is one of Marek's attempts to be funny," Katherine tells everyone and they force a smile.

"*Shlong* is a perfectly good German word," he protests.

"Oh, Marek, stop being silly!" she chides, reddening.

"It is important, what could be more, this question of manhood? Puny or well-hung? To be or not to be?" he asks.

"It isn't funny, Marek," she grumbles, putting an end to it.

But not all his stonemen are so amusing. These he works on, just look how sorrow-sick, weary, dumb with grief, the suffering *in* the stone worn down and shaped by sun and sand, wind and rain, ocean waters. That happens over time.

Mournful as the overcast afternoon, Marek and Katherine had found the stones amongst hundreds strewn between cliff and sea; the day he grew faint from fright and gulls swooped low, warning.

*

Walking by the sea, Marek and Katherine stopped short, bewildered. Blown-out tires, an old bar fridge, a gas range, litter, the exposed beach at low tide. "Where have all these castaways come from?" she asks, but of course he also wants to know. She takes him by the arm and they pick their way among empty seed casings and clumps of yellow-brown seaweed snaked across their path in strands, Medusa's tresses, then stop again to look around, taking in the scene. Above the strewn junk, gliding gulls squawk and a sandpiper scuttles past on stilt-legs hinged backward. Suddenly, the earth tilting, spinning.... A dizzy spell, Marek thinks, passing his hands over his eyes. But no, the clump of seaweed at his feet quivers, shifts and swells, undulating. A sound, at first innocent as the keening of cicadas on a summer's eve, then intruding, insistent, blocking out the ocean's roar, the seagulls' squawk ... like a *grogger*, Purim noisemaker, metal, you twirl it fast. Katya hears it too!

At once the mound heaves, and perfectly camouflaged by the yellow-brown-green colour of kelp, a snake shoots its head upward! Draws back, preparing to strike, stares them down, rattles growing louder, upper jaw pulled up, face made sharp and arrow-like by deep pits on either side from eye to nostril. Its body slithers smooth as rain on satin, its massive coils uncoiling. A *rattlesnake* on the beach?

Marek hears Katya's sharp intake of breath, the snake's rattles *clack-clack-clacking* like the revving of an engine, sounding over breaking waves and seagulls' cries, stifling the scream in his throat. The pits in its face radiate hot fire, its tongue flicks, fangs bared, its yellow sloe eyes breathe evil. He's seen the Gorgon Medusa herself, and is turned to stone.

His grip on Katya's arm tightens ... her heavy breathing ... serpent's rattles *grog-grogging* ... coils sidling, seaweed undulating.... He grows weak, his chest squeezes, and then she's pulling at him, jolting him out of inaction. Together they run. Making its way toward them across the sand, a jeep pulls alongside and a blond young man in a wet suit calls out, "Hi there!" So American! ... and flashes a smile white as seagulls. "You all right, sir?" he asks, seeing Marek so pale and shaky. "We're warning people not to walk in that," he says, and points to the kelp, then tells them the storm last night washed everything down from the river, junk, driftwood, bullfrogs, turtles ... rattlesnakes. "Won't last long in salt water, but we'll have 'em outa here before then," he assures.

"Really!" Katherine exclaims.

Then he knocks twice on the outside of the jeep door, saying, "Take care now," and drives off.

Relieved, they laugh and laugh and start up toward dry sand clear of seaweed and debris. "Ah! It's *extraooo*-rd'nary!" Katherine exults. They will have a good story to tell! Holding hands, they walk on for a bit then pause, again taking everything in. The sunless sky hangs low, overcast, and seamless joins with the sea, vast and flat grey, the colour of slate. Marek squints, peering out at the water, searching for ... what? A glimmer of caring. Does he have to tell you he finds none?

So much life in the ocean! Sea bass and flounder, shark and shrimp, starfish and anemones, and far below the surface, yellow and pink coral *teeming* with life! Even at night, before a storm, the froth on breakers *glows*, a green iridescence shooting like mercury across the water. "So much life, Marek!" Katya exclaims, giving voice to his thoughts. So much *life*.... But when the sun is not out to light his imagination, he cannot see it.

A helicopter flies low over the ocean, making its chop-chop-churning sound, and hovers, a hummingbird. Taking Katya by the arm and avoiding the kelp, he walks back over water-darkened sand toward the ocean's edge and watches their footsteps make mudprints, then fill up. A molted snakeskin remains and someone has built a sand castle with those new turret-like moulds, recently he would think, since it's still intact, and left bucket and shovel behind. In great white letters painted on boulders in sandstone cliffs, some gravity-defying tagger has left his message: *Kato Kalin for President!* "I can only tell you, I love it! Ah! I can breathe!" Marek exults, taking it all in. Washed-up seashells crunching underfoot, they once more head up toward dry sand.

It was here Marek collected stones, between cliff and sea where sleek seals sun themselves on rocks and people look out toward the horizon for dolphins and the spouting of a whale. Here, where hundreds of stones and countless pebbles cushion gull and tern and the feet of men walking the beach as Marek does. He'd felt these once-rough rocks in his palm and remembered how his father and mother so long ago took him to the cemetery in Lwow to his grandparents' grave.... *Here lies Anna and Louis Wronski, Beloved Mother and Father....* How after a moment of silent communion they searched the grounds for stones and finding each their own, approached and placed them on the headstone ... one, two, three, four, five ... six, seven, eight.... Calling cards, to be counted: This many, Anna and Louis, this many on your A list.

This gnaws at him: Where to leave his visiting card for *them,* his own mother and father? Sisters? Brothers? Aunts and Uncles and Cousins? All of them? Where place this marker?

No way for them to know who can be counted on.

No way to say, "I remember."

Late at night, words failing, and fearing sleep, or awaking in a sweat, Marek will again sit at his desk, pencil in hand, hunched over his lists, analyzing, pulling names together from here and there. And his stonemen? They are what they are, stones gathered at a beach, random findings from field and forest, glued together into some kind of order.

What's Going On Here, Anyway?

"YOU SAY FUNNY THINGS LIKE, 'Look, kid, you can't leave me now, I just lost a button off my shirt,' or, 'I've got a freezer full of chicken soup....' It's an incredible thing, an interesting experience. Two people sit and talk quietly, calmly, in low voices to each other about death and dying. I'm not too happy, but you wouldn't notice. Well, maybe. It makes quite a story."

It's been raining, crying, for three days, as though the earth has shrunk to a knowable embracing size, as if Leon were enwrapped and enclosed by the ceiling which is the sky, and the dark sky and thick moving swaying drooping wall of trees, and their sighing and the angry final clap of thunder, the startled lightning, are all close and intimate, possessing human feeling so that his grief seems only one small part of the world's sorrow. It's an incredible thing.

Everything about his wife's surroundings belied the horror of her state: crisp ironed sheets, lacy pillow-slips, eyelet duvet; the honeyed fruitwood four-poster in which she rested; on the dresser, Venetian-crystal miniature perfume bottles, wine and raspberry, dusty rose and trillium blue; chintz flower-printed easy-chair in which Leon sat watching Shirley. She lay propped against pillows, looking straight ahead, neither to one side or the other, her eyes uncannily deep and dark and brooding, vacuous, except for rare moments when she laughed at something funny.

Friends came and went. From the balcony the sun streamed in and spread across her jaundiced face, sunken and high-cheek-boned, once fleshy; neck-muscles thick, skin surrendered, hair thin, lips and jaw retreated, buck-toothed; it's an incredible thing. She said, "The doctor says all I have to think about is getting better." She lay propped against pillows. On the wall opposite the bed where they've always slept was a large oil landscape — frozen lake and snow embankment, jagged rock, and Evergreen — winter-browns and greys and hoary north-country skies, the hard edge of Lauren Harris. Friends came and went, sat and talked quietly, calmly in low voices, ignoring death and dying. "Are you going to serve brisket?" Shirley wanted to know. She lay against lacy pillow-slips, under a flour-white sheet crisply turned back onto flour-white eyelet. Leon thought Shirley would choke on her own body fluids. The nurse wanted to give her something to ease her breathing. A sweet smell, perfume and powder, filled the room; on the dresser, dusty rose and trillium scent bottles, ivory hand-mirror, brush and comb. Her hand lay gracefully on the eyelet, nails manicured and buffed and polished with clear. "I don't feel well, Rhonda," she said, though her friend's name is Frieda. "Not well. The doctor says I have to concentrate on getting better."

Sweet fragrance, over-powdered and perfumed, the nurse has thought to cover the smell of dying. Lining the dresser, crystal scent bottles, old rose and raspberry. The sun shone in from the balcony and onto Shirley lying against lacy pillow-slips and under crisp linens; she turned back to stare at the landscape on the wall opposite, muted browns and greys and tired white, the dark of her eyes bottomless; her manicured hand, nails buffed and polished in clear, lay gracefully on top of the coverlet. Leon, in the flower-printed bedroom chair watched his wife. They sat and talked quietly, calmly, in low voices to one another, an incredible thing. "Are you going to serve brisket?" Shirley asked.

Leon moved forward to hear Frieda who sat on the closed lid of a portable toilet on the far side of Shirley's bed. He wasn't too happy, but you wouldn't notice. On the dresser, medicine vials and needles primly laid out on a towel; on the wall, the frozen lake. "Cold cuts, potato salad, cole slaw ... on trays from the Deli," Frieda answered.

"I'm not well, Rhonda," Shirley said, though her friend's name is Frieda. "Will you make the brisket?" Shirley wanted to know.

Leon leaned forward in his chair, "I've got a freezer full of chicken soup."

"It was smart of me to order things already made up," Frieda remarked, pleased.

"The doctor says all I have to do now is get better," Shirley said. Someone has thought to perfume and powder over the smell of sickness. Her hair, though the scalp showed through, was neatly brushed, her skin ghostly clear and stretched tight across the cheek bones, and her teeth were bucked, too large for her mouth and face which was shrunken. Leon thought she'd choke on her own body fluids. "I have to get better," Shirley said.

She lay very still, her trunk and legs under the light covers mere indentations, so frail she hadn't enough bulk, without support, to keep from collapse. The nurse wanted to turn her over on her side. Shirley's eyes, the irises, were black holes, her expression pleasant and unperturbed. "I guess seventy-one is a long time," she said.

"I need a button on my shirt," Leon said, leaning in.

Laid out on the dresser were rows of medicine bottles and a hypodermic. The nurse wanted to give her something. Opposite the four-poster on which Shirley lay was a frozen lake and hoary skies. "What a smart idea to serve brisket on trays made up at the Deli!" Shirley said, excited.

"A smart idea," Leon agreed.

He thought to get under the covers with her but her legs

might break. He had a way of deeply furrowing his brow and flaring his nostrils; his pitch rises with the phrase and he stresses the words at sentence end, punching the last or next-to-last as though his meaning should be obvious to any idiot; he shows impatience, a way of talking, listen-up! "I just lost a button off my shirt!" A way of talking. "My wife's brother Will's late wife's sister Millie from Szmerna-Herzegovina makes the best brisket," he commented.

"I ordered from the Deli," Frieda told him.

"I'm not well, Frieda," Shirley whispered, "I have to get better."

"How clever to do that," he said and stopped to stare at Frieda seated on the commode.

"I'm sorry, I guess seventy-one years is a long time," Shirley said in a whisper.

Everything in her surroundings belied her plight, over-perfumed and over-powdered as if to cover a rancid odour.

"I lost a button and I have a freezer-full of soup!" Leon protested, angry, his eyes bugged out. He had a way of pulling himself up and sniffing in, nostrils flared, brow furrowed into a deep V, his chin jutted forward, his gaze thrust upward at some non-specific point.

"It's clever of you," Shirley said.

"To order in," Frieda agreed.

"From now on, that's exactly what I'm going to do!" Shirley exclaimed, a sudden burst of light in her eyes.

Leon, on the chintz bedroom chair leaned in. "What's going on here, anyway!" he cried, furrowing his brow, his nostrils flaring.

From the commode, Frieda looked at Shirley, at the manicured nails polished in clear. With tiny movement, slow precision, she picked imaginary lint pills from the coverlet. "I'm going to die, you know," Shirley said.

"Yep, I know," Leon answered, and looked away at the frozen lake. She didn't die in her sleep. At the end she was comatose.

Furrowing his brow into a deep V, Leon looked old, and in a kind of monologue spoke quietly to his wife. "On balance, we had a good fifty years together ... a good marriage. I was less than perfect."

After the end, in a kind of monologue, Leon spoke quietly. "No, she didn't die in her sleep. Well, in her sleep ... what does that mean? Doctors can't relieve the pain of an intelligent person who wants to communicate certain things before they die and needs to, but can't and knows it." Looking old, Leon spoke of his wife, trying to communicate self-evident things any idiot should understand. "She would have preferred some-one less negative. I was less than a perfect mate in a less than perfect institution." Listen up. "On balance, we had a good fifty years together ... a good marriage. She had better taste than I did, you know, and she always ended up being right. The only thing ended up not being right was the dinnerware. I said I liked it because I thought she did, and she said okay because she thought I liked it ... so," he chuckled, "we got something neither of us wanted."

She was comatose near the end. The doctor and Leon discussed how to get through the next hours. Leon thought she would choke on her own body fluids. The nurse wanted to give her something but she might die right away. A sweet smell filled the room, the over-ripe smell of the dying. On top of the dresser were vials and needles, scent bottles, dusty rose and trillium. On the wall opposite, a landscape of the frozen north. You could hear the rattle in her lungs, which wasn't an easy thing. Under the covers his wife's body and legs seemed mere indentations. The nurse wanted to turn her over on her side. His brow in a deep V, looking old, Leon leaned in to his wife and spoke in a kind of monologue. "On the whole, we had a good fifty years together ... a good marriage. I should have been less negative," Leon said. A person speaks quietly, calmly, trying to communicate. Doctors can't relieve the pain.

In the next room the doctor and Leon talked over their

strategy for the next hours. They call it a death rattle, which wasn't an easy thing to hear. The doctor wanted to give her something. "It won't be necessary," the nurse stated evenly. His wife was always right. *You won't be able to deal with this, Leon. I'll just solve this one for you. It's enough. It's time.* "It wasn't an easy thing, there were certain things she wanted to say and knew in her mind, but couldn't. An intelligent person needs to communicate," Leon cried. "Look, kid, you can't leave me now." That's exactly what I'm going to do, he heard.

It's an incredible thing, an interesting experience. "I'm not too happy, but you wouldn't notice. Well, maybe." The room was filled with the sweetness of death, and the sound of rain on the balcony, and on the leaves that hang heavy, continued as though he'd said nothing more significant than that the weather was dismal. On the dresser was her ivory-handled mirror. "Everything I touch or smell reminds me, even the upholstery on the couch. She had better taste than I did. The only thing ended up not being right was the dinnerware." He was going to cry and stopped talking. He had a way of punching the last or next-to-last word as though arguing or lecturing, "It's an incredible thing," begging you to understand. "Neither of us wanted it."

"I'm going to die, you know," she said quietly.

"Yep, I know." He looked old, speaking softly about death and dying. He had a way of talking. "My late-wife Shirley's sister Bela…"

The night was heavy with rain, nothing unusual, just another rainy evening, establishing his grief as only one microscopic part of the world's sorrow. "I guess seventy-one years is a long time," he said. "I'm not too happy, but you wouldn't notice. Well, maybe."

Out to Lunch with the Girls

"**I**F YOU LIVE TO BE A HUNDRED, you'll never be like your father!" Hannah blurted out to Sammy who stood towelling dry his hair. Not angry at first, too stunned, he just stared at her, his raised arm frozen. Everyone around the pool quit talking and, not believing what they'd heard, turned to look at Hannah.

Upset, more than upset, Hannah finally lashed out at her son. That's the way it all started, Hannah thinks, sitting alone. I told him I wanted to leave, how many times did I have to say it? I'd get home on my own if I could, but no, I have to ask. Years ago I should have learned to drive, now it's too late. For everything.

From her deck chair Hannah gazes at silhouettes etched against the sun, stretching like paper cutouts along the sand bar, a ribbon in the sea. No, not the sea; *its* waters are turbulent, as youth; the Gulf flows calm, still as the aged, as Hannah. Outlined by throbbing heat, children dig, fat ladies, bent forward, search for sea-shells, their big bottoms full moons spurning Hannah; side-view, men with hilly bellies supervise, or stare at the horizon into the sun, legs apart, feet planted, arms akimbo, wings. Hannah takes it all in.

Well, that's when the *argument* started, a few hours ago; actually the whole unhappy affair began early this morning when Sammy, her eldest, called. "Ma? I'm coming by to pick you up. The kids are coming over, you'll spend a few hours."

As she reflects back on the day Hannah sighs, the chronic sigh of swells carried shoreward in slithering licks toward the beach line. Nothing stays the same, she thinks, looking down at fingers once long and fine; knotted and misshapen now from "arthur itis" they can barely hold a pencil, though she still writes letters asking for donations, *Save The Children*, the words shaky, running downhill. She's proud she can manage.

What a glorious day, remarkable, Hannah whispers; no matter what's happened since this morning. A warm breeze cools her old body. She's seventy-eight, eighty-one really. She tells friends: My sons guess ... seventy-eight, eighty, eighty-one, eighty-two.... They think the older I am, the better I'm doing. Go figure it out, at this age. When she met Al fifty-six years ago — thirteen years he's gone now — it wasn't so good marrying an "older" woman, so she made up she was younger. *Three years, he never knew, it didn't hurt him.*

At one time, when she and Al were young, Hannah's hair fell over sloping milk white shoulders in long chestnut-brown curls kissing the slope of her breast, all very feminine; her dresses, gauzy and flowing, brushed her ankles. Now the *hair* is milk-white; shoulders stooped, she has shrunk, is frail where once she'd been imposing, threatening in middle age, no longer. She strokes her slacks at the thigh and smiles at the thought of herself, an old woman in track-soled running shoes, holding onto her son's arm, *her* arm trembling on his, a cat's purring. At this age Hannah avoids mirrors; her nose, its large nostrils flared back, has spread more, appears even longer, flatter, and the lines alongside thin straight lips have deepened, dig sharply down to the jaw so that when she speaks her mouth and shortened chin open and shut like a wood dummy. How silly looking she's become.

This is the woman people see, but Al, if he was living.... "You're still some sexy babe!" he used to say. "Just like the first time I spotted you with your friend Tillie in the Hot Shoppe. Nate — you remember him? — an' me walked in, cruisin' around...." Oh, he was naughty! Hannah laughs to herself. Gave me a little slap on the bottom when he talked like that — not in front of anyone! — and chuckled and puffed on that smelly fat cigar I hated. My children, Sammy and Martin, see only what they see.

But no one can call her slant eyes an old woman's: half-moons, lucid green, hot ice. When she sets her lips in obstinacy, fleshy cheek bones rise and underline eyes gleaming with an inner hotness like those of a zealot. Al used to say they were the eyes of the devil. No, that much about her is not foolish.

"That would be nice, Sammy," she replied this morning. What else could I say? she asks herself. How could she tell Sammy she'd miss 2 Live Crew on Face the Nation? She had waited all week to hear Miss Florida confront them on this Women and Pornography issue. Rappers they're called ... rappers, rapping ... so many strange new words. And then Sammy phoned.

Each week after Face the Nation everyone gathers in the common room for Sing Along With Ernestine; by the time that ended Josephina would be back from Sunday Mass and they'd all go out to lunch. That had been Hannah's plan, but she couldn't tell that to Sammy; she's forever complaining she doesn't see him and the children enough.

Oh, she did tell Sammy in her own way, Hannah remembers. He picked her up at ten this morning. If she managed things right she could be back by one o'clock, in time for lunch. "I want to leave now, Sammy," she'd said after two hours had gone by. Hannah had said that very clearly: "I'm tired."

She wasn't tired. Not at all. The truth is she didn't want to sit any longer at Sammy's observing others DO, while she, Hannah, watched, doing what she'd always done, listen to Sammy, Grace, the grandchildren, go along, devote her attention to them as if she had no life of her own. Well, it's my own fault, she chastises. Hasn't she always given herself to the children? Her time, thoughts, precious possessions, wanting as much as she had, her children's love? The samovar brought from

Romania, her sister's Victorian bar pin, swatches of fine lace crocheted by Hannah's grandmother. Hannah had enjoyed the giving, the look on their faces. But where, where all those years after Al died was the return?

They were busy. All children are busy. Sammy lived so far away, Alberta before he and his family moved to Florida, and Martin not so far, Ottawa. Martin's a businessman, a *macher*, always on the run — drives into the city from the Gatineau, flies to New York, Chicago, Vancouver. Used to "drop in" to Toronto four, five times a year on his way from one deal to another. Stayed a few hours and ran. Oh, they called: *How are you, Mom? We're fine, the kids are doing good …* and on about their work, the weather, one of the children with a cold. But she didn't want that, she wanted letters. Letters meant the writer took the time. *Letters I can read over and over.* But Martin said people today use the telephone, nobody writes letters anymore.

The sun cuts its path, a laser, through the waters of the Gulf as if allowing Hannah, like Moses, to walk to the horizon and disappear into the heavens. It's a wonder God didn't take me long ago, she thinks. How is it I'm still here?

Hannah's been asking since Al died, but God never answers. Sammy, Martin, her friends, don't answer either. But she doesn't mind, it's what she *feels*. Al did me dirty, she tells them. When I can't sleep — two, three, four in the morning — I talk to him. Why did you desert me? I ask; not so much any more.

Never in all her days did she think she could get along without Al. But after thirteen years she's come to like deciding things for herself, spending her own money, signing checks … even buying groceries. Al had done that too, she didn't drive. Who would've thought she'd have this new life?

Her question hangs in air, eternal and unanswered as the crash of ocean breakers, carried with them out to sea. All those years with him. He'd been ill for so long, six years — the Big C-word Hannah still can't bring herself to say — and she'd seen him through, never letting on how serious it was. *Did he know?* He never said, but his eyes told all that words could never.

Where were the children then? With their own families, what did she expect? Letters, maybe. Paper children. And after? Years of silence, talking to Albert at two in the morning, *Who gave you the right to go first? These long hours, what will I do with them? Nobody should know such loneliness. Where are all the people we did so much for?* The clock's pendulum swinging, its ticks and tocks making time something Hannah could grasp, something solid. Hannah listened for Albert's voice but there was only the silence and the tick-tocking. She'd done her share of crying where no one saw or heard. "Oh, Honey, you'll never know, it's no fun getting old, alone," she told anyone listening.

It was her sons' idea to move. She'd been angry at first. After so many years without Al she'd eventually grown used to it, developed her own life rhythm. Snoozed part of the day, something she never let on to *anyone,* watched *ABC, NBC, CBC,* read magazines, wrote asking for donations to *Save the Children,* and met friends at Fran's for lunch. But they began dying off, her eyesight wasn't so good anymore, and she'd fallen once or twice, lost her balance walking. Too old to be living alone, that's what Sammy and Martin said, and so they packed up her things while she cried, made empty despairing noises, *Why am l here? How come God let me live this long? I should be dead, with Al. I never wanted to be a burden,* and fussed over years of accumulated precious junk: faded sepia snapshots in shoe-boxes grown dusty in the closet; the black velvet beret that had been so stylish; paint-by-number clowns Al did when he'd been sick. What was she to do with all this, who would want these things? Who wanted *her?*

Now, in the December of her life, instead of barren trees Hannah drinks in lush waxy palms. Remarkable, just remarkable, she says aloud as if seeing them for the first, or last time, and knowing it. Living near her eldest son, she is contented here. *The Second Chance Retirement Community.* Hannah calls it *The Last Chance,* thinks that more accurate. Sammy and Martin chose this place so she could be near Sammy, and because she could afford it. Well, Sammy and Martin have to help. She hates that, having to take from them, ask for money to buy a gift, a dress, get her hair done. She isn't used to asking anymore. What went wrong?

Sammy thinks her new companions strange. Who is *he* to say? *He's* strange, a queer duck. But Hannah's new friends, strange as they are, have accepted *her*, that's the important thing, and Hannah has *chosen* to accept them. It hadn't been Hannah's wish to leave Toronto and all she loved: lunches at the Art Gallery with Hadassah women — oh, the music she'd heard in its grand vestibule — piano, flute, harp — and the great curving sculpture outside, smooth and round and open, *feminine*, the children climbing up and around and through... Not *her* idea to move after eighty years in the same city to an unknown place, beautiful as it is, leave old friends, make new ones. She could have gone to *Baycrest*. Now she's here in Florida. She was told to make a new life, and she has. With Josephina, Pat, Gertrude and Bertie.

*

They are seated around their table at breakfast in the Retirement dining room. Hannah picks over her food, oatmeal cold, bread stale, coffee from the bottom of the pot. Her frizzed head jutting into Hannah's face, Josephina grins, a wide gummy gap between her front teeth, beagle brown eyes pleading, a soulful hag. "Want to see my ring? It's from my sister, the nun," thrusting her hand under Hannah's nose, pointing to the gold body of Christ circling her finger. Hannah barely looks down; she's seen the ring a hundred times before. "Very nice," she says dryly.

There's not much humour in Josephina, or Bertie for that matter. Bertie's too high-strung. Sometimes when Hannah finds her in the television parlour, Bertie stares, not at the set, but someplace no one else sees. Her high cheek bones intimidate — this is someone on the edge — push against stretched pale skin and below pale lost eyes. But other times Bertie is all twittery, and her eyes burn and she talks excitedly, up close, nose to nose. Still, they have some good laughs together.

A cigarette between Bertie's fingers curls smoke into the air, bothers Hannah. As if that, Josephina's annoying drivel, and the pasty oatmeal aren't enough, Gertrude lets out a resounding belch.

"Uh, I'm sorry, Hannah don't like me to burp," she says, glancing at the others.

"I don't think it's right. After all, we're trying to eat," Hannah snaps.

"I can't help it," Gertrude says. Her face has a characteristic twisted look, her body lumpy although not unduly large, and the whole of her bears an awkwardness as if in putting the parts together someone's made a mistake in the assembling. "It just comes out," she finishes.

"If she was in India," Pat offers, "it would be a compliment."

"Yeah?" Gertrude asks, pleased.

"Well, she's not in India," Hannah counters. "She's in Florida."

"So? They don't belch in Florida? They're all from Philly and New Jersey," Pat remarks. "They ain't so hoity-toity."

"And Canada," Bertie adds very seriously.

"*They're* too polite for that," Hannah says.

"She don't like my snorin' either," Pat says to Gertrude. The words come from small heart-shaped lips, rouged, moving in the midst of doughy flesh pale as flour, three hundred pounds, a sack. Crochet needles momentarily stop their flurrying. "Last night I fell asleep in here watchin' the TV and next thing I know I feel a WHACK and hear somebody screamin', 'YOU'RE SNORING! STOP IT!' It's her, Hannah. She threw her slippers at my back! You scared the hell outa me!" Pat says to Hannah.

"You're always falling asleep in the TV room. I couldn't hear my program," Hannah defends herself.

"I can't help it," Pat says.

"But my goodness, it's so loud! How can a person hear?" Hannah demands.

"Well, you do somethin', you think I don't know, but you do it!" Pat, smiling, winks at the others. "You give it out."

"From the other end!" Gertrude exclaims, catching on. Hannah's breath catches and her eyes, sheepish, look up from half-closed lids. She starts to respond but not knowing how, stops. "At least mine comes out the good end!" Gertrude finishes, satisfied.

"Yeah, you really send 'em up! You think I'm sleepin' when I'm not and I hear you! WHOMP!" Pat accompanies this with an upward thrust of her fist and massive arm.

"Fat Pat," Hannah whispers under her breath. But they all laugh, and laugh and laugh, Hannah included. She feels like a *real* person, not Hannah, Albert's wife, Sammy's mother, Hannah, *Grandmother*.

"Well never mind, we'll all go out to lunch. After Josephina gets back from Mass. We'll get George to take us in the van to Denny's." Pat returns to her crocheting.

That was at breakfast before Sammy picked Hannah up, one thing led to another and she hurled awful words at her son. By the time she got back from Sammy's, Josephina had returned from Mass and they'd all left, without Hannah. Instead, she sits on the red-striped deck chair, alone, an old woman in slacks and running shoes, staring out at the Gulf, watching the sun drop in the sky, turning over in her mind the day's events.

*

At her son's home, a Florida-style ranch on a canal, Hannah, her daughter-in-law Grace, granddaughter Mary, and Joe, gather around the pool. It's hot. Hannah sits tight-kneed in a canvas deck chair under the patio umbrella, dabs at her neck and throat with a linen handkerchief and periodically checks her watch. She plans to stay until noon then leave just in time for lunch.

Mary and Joe's four-year-old, JB, tilts back onto the heels of new rattlesnake cowboy boots, clumps about, a storm of energy, showing off. In tight jeans, his lean little-boy's body swaggers, runs, twists, falls. Furtively, he raises eyes bright as polished rock, a lustrous brown-gold cat's-eye, checks who's looking, scoots back up, on the move again. Hannah is exhausted watching, and loses her heart.

"Come on tiguh, thiats enough, naow," Joe drawls as he sweeps JB into his arms. "Let's get yew into thiat there pool."

"Can I get you anything, Mom?" Grace asks. Grace always asks Hannah, very solicitous.

Grace has been especially kind to Hannah since her move to Florida, Hannah has to admit, very warm and generous. Grace is that kind of person. But she and Hannah had had their problems. No doubt Grace still remembers, memory like an elephant, never lets go. It's not healthy to be like that.

Al said things he probably never should have, but Grace claims he made accusations Hannah can't recall. *What's the matter, Sammy, you* gotta *marry this girl? She trap you inta somethin'?* Why wouldn't her Albert be upset with the marriage? Hannah's eyes flash even now, so long after. He and Hannah were never synagogue-goers, but a *shiksa?*

It was Grace, it's true, who asked Hannah about Rosh Hashanah, Yom Kippur, Chanukah, Passover, and Grace who asked for the Jewish Cookbook. That's where Hannah made the mistake. Hannah didn't know that much about the holidays from the Torah point of view, but she ought to have given Grace her copy of *The Theodore Herzl Hadassah Group's "Fiddlin' in the Kitchen."* Hannah sighs. *It's all my fault the girl became anorexic; not a spot of flesh you could noodle.* Although, Grace *is* somewhat better now; put on a little weight, the bones not so alone.

Since that time in the beginning when Al made those slurs — maybe he *had* gone too far — not everything ran smoothly between Grace, Sammy and Hannah. Still...

"Mom? Can I get you anything?" Hannah hears Grace repeat, interrupting her thoughts.

"No, no dear, I'm just fine," Hannah replies with a wave-like gesture of her hand and a glance at her watch.

Grace goes into the kitchen to prepare some lunch. Hannah did not want lunch, she was going *out* to lunch. At one time she would have jumped to help Grace in the kitchen. Not anymore. Hannah's learned. Sometimes she offers, she *asks*. "I don't mind," Grace once responded, "I think I've finally convinced myself your helping isn't a criticism."

Hannah's relieved Grace has come to that. Feeling useful is important to Hannah, that goes without saying. Can she sit and not *do* when she could be in the kitchen making blintzes? Frankly though, Grace's sense of her disapproval is not unfounded. Grace's housekeeping is disastrous. Not so bad now she's restricted her hobbies to the bedroom. What a room! Forget it! Make-up, sticky candy wrappers, paperbacks, newspapers, needlepoint, dried flowers, recycled paper, scissors and glue, hairbrushes sprouting tangled strands, strewn blouses — bright yellow and green flowery affairs — shoes everywhere. Hopeless, that's all Hannah can say.

By the pool Hannah's granddaughter Mary smokes while watching her son JB in the water, his chest plopped across a rubber inner-tube, thrashing his arms in front, kicking his legs inside the doughnut's centre. Mary's a chain-smoker, a dirty habit. Hannah wishes she'd stop, but she keeps her mouth shut.

"Joe's going to school to learn a trade, Grandmom, did you hear? Installing heating units."

What kind of *lemmishkeh* learns heating in Florida? Hannah bites her lip. *Once the milk's spilt....*

"Driving the truck kept him away too much," Mary goes on.

"We're getting married soon, did Daddy tell you? Joe wants it. JB's four now. It'll be the Sunday after Christmas."

"That's nice," Hannah smiles, checking her watch, thinks: A *granddaughter*, talks like it was an immaculate conception, that's what the *goyim* call it. So much *goyishe*! *Goyishe* mess, *goyishe* cooking, *goyishe* names. And Mary's got a *goyishe kop*! Hannah knocks her own head as if talking aloud. How did Sammy allow all this?

"We're being married in our home, Grandmom," Mary tells her.

She's not getting the family sterling, certainly not! Hannah stews. There used to be a name ... *mistress*! What can I say? *Sorry, dear, for being late with my gift, time flies so. No sooner's the baby born, it's time for a wedding present!* Ridiculous!

"Not in church?" In front of the Christmas tree and under the picture of Mother Mary and Baby Jesus? "By a Rabbi?" Hannah asks aloud, pointedly, she can't help herself.

Hannah long ago became resigned to her son having married Grace, one of *them*, but she's never forgiven Sammy for the way he and Grace brought up the children, she out of ignorance, he out of spite. Just one queer duck, that's what my son is, she tells others with a wry twist of her lips. Do my grandchildren know anything about Chanukah or the High Holydays, or about *kosher*? We always mixed meat and dairy, Albert and me, but do Sammy's children even *know* they're not supposed to? Hannah's youngest, Martin, told her to M.Y.O.B., Mind Your Own Business.

"No, not by a Rabbi, by an Ecumenical Minister," Sammy puts in. "What're you checking your watch for, Ma?"

"I'm getting tired, Sammy, I want to go," Hannah answers.

"You're always complaining we're running off. Where're *you* running? Sit a little. I'm going to take a quick dip. Here I come, JB, Grandpop's coming, yes I am!" Sammy shouts in his singsong reserved for children.

Hannah's going to be late. Josephina will be getting back from Mass, then she and the others will wait a few minutes and leave without her. Hannah taps her track-shoed foot and, unseeing, flips through the pages of one of Grace's glossy women's magazines. Hannah will have to hold her annoyance in check. How can she tell Sammy all this nonsense about children and fathers and weddings has become tiresome and she wants to go out to lunch with the girls?

Hannah fidgets her body, looks once again at her watch and drops the magazine onto a table. "I want to go, Sammy, I told you I'm getting tired!" Towelling his hair dry, water dripping from his peppery beard, Sammy says irritably, "Okay, okay, Mom. Don't be in such a rush."

He was paying no attention. Just the way Al used to be. She told Al throughout their marriage: We don't *need* another new car, you just bought this one! Didn't want to take a trip to Montreal before he died, didn't *want* to be dragged all over the place. I'm too old for that, she told him. He hadn't listened. In the end she always did what Albert wanted, gave in, no sense fighting it.

Neither does Sammy listen. Not my younger son Martin either, she thinks. And I shouldn't have listened to *them*.

"Look, Ma. About your building going Condo ... I'm not letting you buy in, and *I'm* not putting money in, it's too risky," Sammy had said. "Just go on renting the place, let somebody else put their own money up."

That was a while back, after Al had been dead ten years, but Sammy and Martin treat her the same today. She pictures Martin nodding in agreement with Sammy, hears him.

"Frankly Mom, I don't have time right now to look into it. Sammy's right. Rent."

"I've got my own money, I can do it without you," Hannah remembers saying stubbornly. She's angry just thinking about it, clenches her fists, her chest expands. Hannah's bosom has grown larger over the years, she doesn't know how it got so big.

"No, Ma, you don't have enough. Listen to us, we wouldn't steer you wrong."

Well, she doesn't care *what* Martin said, she'd been too old to worry about being forced from her apartment.

And now she wants to leave. She wants to go out to lunch with the girls. Maybe Al hadn't listened about a lot of things but he was attentive. Romantic, a gentleman. Remember Hannah, remember the time Al hid money under the rug, it made such a lump you tripped over it? He was saving for a present he said, a surprise. What a guy!

No, Sammy was not like his father *that* way. He'd never have his father's charm, the way he used to make her laugh: *Do you want to see the moon, Hannah!* jokingly, scowling, pretending anger over something she'd said. Sammy doesn't see her enough as a woman, a real person, to tease like that.

And so, these thoughts piling one upon the other as she fidgeted, tapped her foot, flipped through her magazine and checked the time, Hannah had gotten mad and that's when she blurted, "If you live to be a hundred you'll never be like your father!" That's when Sammy's arm stopped in mid-air, and he went pale, stared at Hannah, and everyone fell silent.

"What's wrong, Grandmom?" JB's high-up voice cut through, "Daddy, what's wrong with Mom-mom?"

Hannah set her lips. She had nothing else to say.

*

Staring out onto the darkening gulf, its waters moody purple, Hannah twists her handkerchief, her hands trembling, pushes her legs firmly together. She admonishes herself: Such a foolish old lady! A second chance, truly, new friends, Fat Pat and crazy Josephina, Sammy and Martin so good — *and* Grace — a granddaughter nearby, little JB .... To walk outside anytime, feel the sun on her bare arms, see the shimmering Gulf, the beach, palm trees... Remarkable. She is very lucky. Yes. That's what she tells everyone. Why then does she feel this way? Tears well up, she twists the handkerchief tighter. The still-glistening path through the water narrows to the sun; the last chance, Hannah whispers. At this low slant it washes palms and beach, the few remaining figures along the sand bar and Hannah herself with deep gold making the world around her achingly mysteriously beautiful; idyllic — unicorns and white stallions.

It's turning chilly. The tide is out. Dark and wet and muddy where the water had been, seagulls stand their one-legged guard over pebbles, shells and driftwood, small sculptures. The sun at the horizon burns red-orange, its embers consuming clouds drifting across it, the sky an inferno. Soon the sun will drop off the edge, disappear.

Sammy had driven her back, neither of them speaking. I must have hurt him, Hannah admits. Why didn't I just tell him, "I have someplace to go"? It should have been simple enough. But she didn't, she said she was tired; she *had* to say one thing to get the other. Never mind, Sammy should have listened at the beginning and she shouldn't have to explain anything. These thoughts nag at her.

Hannah *thinks* Sammy knows why she's angry, but she's not certain. He seemed so defenceless, an injured bird, banded seagull. His eyes, *her* eyes, slanted and icy green, looked innocent, confused, and Sammy, her son, looked tired and old. His face clay, sparse hair and beard white, lips thin like Hannah's, the lower receded as if the gums had given out, shoulders sloping, none really, his middle paunchy; on the whole, wearing down. When she closes her eyes Hannah sees Sammy putting on his shirt, buttoning it, his long slender fingers trembling.

I didn't apologize, no, and I won't say I'm sorry because I'm not, Hannah thinks hotly. She imagines herself at Denny's with Josephina, Pat, Gertrude, and Bertie; it's crowded with young couples and noisy children. Pat digs into a stack of syrup-soaked pancakes.

"That don't look like no diet to me," Gertrude digs.

"You're not one to talk," Pat answers and shoots a look at Gertrude's heaped plate. Gertrude shuts up. With a sly glance at Hannah she makes a show of stifling a belch. "See, Hannah, how good I'm bein'?"

Bertie is all fluttery and lights another cigarette; her eyes dart from table to table. She's not used to all this commotion and worries aloud they'll miss the van back. Josephina shows her ring to the waitress, tells about her sister the nun. And they all ask Hannah about *Face the Nation*. "You're the intellectual, Hannah," they say, and to herself Hannah marvels, *ME!*

Her thoughts return to Sammy. And Grace, and the grand-children. Hannah strokes one misshapen hand over the other, then dabs at her eyes; her heart aches so.

I wanted ... why is it so difficult? I wanted *to go out to lunch with the girls.*

Age Appropriate

DEAR DOCTOR TUCKER:
Since my visit with you several months ago, I've been doing some major soul searching. I'm sorry to report that in the weeks following, I behaved like an aging woman abandoned by her husband of many years for the familiar trophy girl. A round of facials, massages, and body wraps did little to alleviate my unhappiness. I raced about, seeking dermatologists and cosmeticians, shopped till I dropped, purchased jars and jars of creams and lotions, anti-wrinkle, anti-aging, lifting, toning, hydrating, and exfoliating. Joined Weight Watchers. A fitness club.

Then one evening I sat down and examined my behaviour. How had I arrived at this fever of discontent? What began in your office as mere annoyance — the prick of a mosquito — swelled by the time I left to the sting of anger. Oh, the cleansing thrill of such a purge! It was the desire to share this infectious pleasure that drove me to write. But what frame of mind could have driven me to you in the first place?

The precise event, Doctor, came during one unsuspecting appointment with my hairdresser, no, *stylist*, given he charges an amount worthy of this elevated title. The stylist wields scissors and comb, brush and blow dryer, with a certain flare, a certain drama to hand and arm movements, not to mention a skillful use of psychology. How else to explain such magical transformations that happen in the salon? A woman walks in with a mousey listless head of hair and leaves under the illusion she's naturally blessed with layers of luxurious locks. Enters a plain Jane, feeling dried out and pallid from winter's punishments and exits with a spark to her eye, smile on her lips, and sprightly spring to her step.

Now, you think I've wandered off course here, Doctor, but rest easy, I haven't. I need you to understand how vital the relationship is between a woman and her stylist, how critical his influence; see what I'm about to relate as the inciting incident it truly was.

Pulling from my handbag a photo taken some ten years back, I asked Vito, my stylist of several decades, "Can you give me a cut like this?"

Vito examined the picture for several seconds.

Smiling into the camera, my face framed by a boy's bob, I beamed up at the lens, cute as a pixie. The bob was shaped quite full at the crown and sides, sharply trimmed around the ears, showing them off, with a stray pointed wisp clipped to emphasize the cheekbones. Bangs brushed the top of my glasses, which were very large, the fad then, and my hair was coloured titian red.

"Well," Vito said at last, "this picture was taken some time ago, before you had wrinkles."

Can you imagine, Doctor Tucker? *Before I had wrinkles!* That coming from Vito? I masked my shock. My dismay.

From where he stood behind me seated in the barber's chair, he gazed at my reflection in the mirror. Cupping my head with his thumb and two fingers on either side, he turned it this way and that, then deftly combed the wet strands back at the ears and down over my forehead. I could see his dubious expression, but I remained sanguine. Vito had a way with women. So Italian! Flirtatious eye, Italian-made silk shirts, loose-fitting black linen designer jackets and hair longish to the nape.

Calmly we discussed a more appropriate hairdo. It wasn't until I returned home that all the self-doubt and hurt I'd bottled up in the salon, and after on the long subway ride, came pouring out. Surprised at seeing his wife crying, apparently over a hair cut, my husband asked what was the matter and on hearing the sorry story exploded like so many (refreshingly) clueless men: "Fire the hairdresser!"

That night, I washed and went straight to sleep, consciously avoiding any studied gazing into the mirror. But I remember the jolt I experienced next morning when, grogging out of bed and into the bathroom, I noticed in the looking glass that Vito was right! A sly dissipation had begun, etching into my image like lye. I drew in closer. Cracks ran, rivulets, above my upper lip; tiny brush strokes feathered out along the lower. Labial creases, cheek to chin. Lacy threads around the eyes, carved "V" between the brows. When, oh when, I asked, did all this happen?

Really, Doctor, does one see this creeping crisis in photographs day-to-day, week-to-week, this year to the next? No, one morning, decades later, we look in the mirror and it hits us, *wap*! I determined the harm hadn't yet reached catastrophic levels, but I'd have to act quickly. I found myself soon after seated in your waiting room, anxiously reading certificates on the wall, testament to your qualifications: Conrad B. Tucker, M.D., University of Toronto School of Medicine; American Board of Facial and Plastic Reconstructive Surgeons; Royal College of Surgeons of Canada in Otolaryngology. Assurances.

Since that time, I've been doing a good deal of thinking, as I said, turning over in my mind the pros and cons of deleting twenty years from my face. Thinking that I owed you this letter, I decided you deserved a stroll through my musings on the dilemma, some insight into nagging questions. During one of our weekly sessions, my therapist challenged me with one that has been bothering me ever since. We'd been discussing relationships (what else?), male, female. Growing older. What did he make of a sixty-year-old man dating a thirty-year-old woman? A sixty-something woman dating a thirty-something man? At one point in the dialogue he raised his glance over the rim of his glasses, his expression sombre, and asked: "What do *you* think? Do you think it age appropriate?"

Age appropriate? I pondered that. In a jarring — how can I express it? — *epiphanic* moment, the thought hit: Wasn't that what Vito was really putting to me? When was something age appropriate — or not? I asked myself. Mini-skirts at seventy? Thongs at fifty? Parkinson's at thirty-five? Sixty-five? Sex at eighty? Fourteen? *Looking* older, showing it?

I heard your name mentioned, Doctor, when eavesdropping on three women seated at a table next to mine in Yorkville's Le Paradis Bistro. They were talking about some repair work you did for a friend of theirs. At first I thought you were a plumber, carpenter, or maybe a roofer, but no, turned out you refurbished faces. The women were attractive, looked to be in their early to mid-forties and were bemoaning their growing state of disrepair. Nose, eyes, chin. Breasts, tummy, thighs. I immediately went home and found you in the phone book. With an office in up-market Hazelton Lanes you had to be respectable, or at least attractive to the well-to-do.

To go back to your Hazleton Avenue waiting room, I think you were so very clever in choosing your receptionist. Just enough plumpness to suggest health, and the correct amount of makeup, subtly applied, for the skin to sparkle. Oh, the brilliance of having a nurse nearby! This in itself was comforting. She was young, I observed. At least I believed so. I searched her arms and hands for brown sunspots, for skin like translucent saran wrap, for blue popping veins. None of that! All body parts matched up, face, trunk, limbs, attesting, like the rings of a seedling, to her youth. Confirming her authenticity. I was looking at the real thing! She was the fresh, bright-eyed babe we remember ourselves being; the possibilities we might yet dream of. She smiled her scarlet smile, settled on me a café-noir gaze and at once the surroundings in your waiting room came into focus, made sense. All was harmonious. This marble-floored, leather-couched office with its glass doors, tasteful paintings and art-deco stainless steel and chrome — a kind of plastic surgeon's show room for putting one's best face forward — promised the best buy for the beauty buck, a grand gift of glamour and eternal youth.

But you already know all this. You probably also had a pretty good idea of how shocked I'd be on seeing my (unsmiling, black and white) image on a computer screen. Why had I not noticed that droop to my right eye before? The "creping" along my cheeks that your nurse so delicately pointed out? My projection on a second screen alongside the first, smiling, in colour, brightly lit and "lifted" — the wrinkle-free virtual me — immediately proclaimed what happy possibilities were mine to purchase.

I examined again the "before" and "after." Nurse must have seen my look of utter dismay. "Don't worry, dear," she said gently. "You can be repaired."

Next thing I knew, I was making a follow-up appointment to see you. I so keenly remember our first meeting a week later because that day it was quite windy and raining hard. I shielded my hair as best I could by pulling the shoulders and collar of my coat up over my head and dashed, quite breathless and rosy from the rain, through your office doors. You were saying goodbye to a patient, a recent one, I assumed, judging from her swaddling bandages.

You glanced over at me with what I thought was an appreciative once-over. I was feeling invigorated, running in from the brisk outside, my complexion ruddy, hair tossed; *young.* Just goes to show you, doctor, how wrong one can be.

Soon we were sitting opposite each another in your private office and you were asking what I was thinking of "having done."

"I was thinking laser. Maybe Botox. Here ... and here ... and here?" I thrust my face slightly forward, pointing to the troublesome places.

"Botox won't do it."

"Maybe laser?"

"You can't laser a few spots. It's all or nothing. You don't want to look blotchy, do you? Besides, why put yourself through all that discomfort without achieving the desired results? Why stop with your lip line and brow?"

"Why not?" I put to you.

You seemed taken aback, Doctor Tucker. "Well," you huffed, "laser ... botox ... whatever ... won't take care of the rest," and here you reached over and with two fingers to my jaw, turned my head side to side.

"What, rest?" I asked.

"The neck. That's what a face lift is. It *lifts* everything that has sagged, dropped, drooped, gone slack," you said, as if I didn't get it the first time. "You see, here, the muscle under the chin. As one ages it loses elasticity, its tone."

Women hadn't the option of camouflage with a nice beard like yours, I offered. You smiled and eased your hand from the jaw line to the area around my eyes — nice eyes, I must say, brown with flashes of gold like maple syrup; and direct, honest.

"A little lift here above the ear and at the temples" — carefully pulling the skin back as you said this. "Of course we'll still need to do some lasering after the lift, for the fine lines."

"Are things that bad?" I asked.

"Don't you want to look your very best for your husband?" you wanted to know.

I glanced quickly at you but detected nothing but the most sincere earnestness. I appreciate the importance of being earnest, so I considered my husband as you advised. Now he's a nice looking man but honestly, Dr. Tucker, he could use a few nips, tucks, and lipo-sucks himself.

"I'm very proud of my work, what I do for women," you said. "I give them a new sense of themselves. They meet the world with re-found confidence. I give them the gift of happiness."

Happy women. Aloud, I said, "Where are all the happy men?"

Your eyes widened, then narrowed. "That day is coming," you finally answered. "More and more are coming in for cosmetic enhancement. Bald men want tufted tops, fat men want abs, small men want inches." You threw me a sidelong glance to see if I caught your meaning. "To feel more powerful, vigorous. To compete in the workplace against the twenty-somethings nipping at their heels."

Aah. I grew thoughtful. "Aren't we talking serious operation? I mean, isn't the lift you're proposing what the Indians call scalping?"

You weren't responding to my scalping question, Doctor Tucker, so I asked, "Won't I experience shock? Oh, it's not only the trauma to my system I worry about. Suppose I look at my 'after' self in the mirror and don't know who I am? I mean, I've grown accustomed to my face." My voice had taken on a nostalgic whimper. "Won't I suffer emotional duress?"

"Do you *want* to?" you asked, your voice challenging.

Do I want to? I wondered, Doctor, if all doctors refer to the same prompt book for standard answers to difficult questions. I say that because of a conversation between a surgeon and a young Filipino nanny of limited English I overheard from my hospital bed at Mt. Sinai at the time of my hysterectomy. Her speech was halting, her voice shaking, as she told him how scared she was, unsure of exactly what parts of her insides he was planning to relieve her of. He replied that the operation was nothing really; she'd have a little discomfort and be as good as — better than — new. "Won't I be depressed after?" she cautiously put to him (her concerned employers had warned her of that).

"Do you want to be depressed? If you don't want to be, you won't be," he finished, putting an end to it.

You must have noted the sequence of emotions playing across my face, Doctor Tucker, calculated the thoughts colliding in my brain, because you didn't wait for my reply.

"My dear," you explained patiently, "purchasing beauty has become a common occurrence. *Everybody's* doing it. Your hairdresser, secretaries, waitresses. There's really nothing to it. A few days of bruising, a week's rest. A little discomfort."

Aha! Those code words again. Do I hear echoes of soothing promises the Mt. Sinai Doctor made to the Philippine girl? A little discomfort. Why, I'd heard those very words from my own doctor at the time I bid good-bye to my womb. Either male GYNs don't know *bubkas* about women's woes, wombs, ovaries and such, or they're — dare I use the "l" word — lying? At the very least, fudging. When you say "discomfort," whoa! — my whole being goes on alert, my eyes bug out, and my hair freaks straight up like a sixties hippie with an Apache cut.

"Aren't you being over-dramatic, Ms. Enfeld? Surgery is becoming so ordinary that one day those who have opted to look their age will be social outcasts."

Social outcasts. Now this brings up an interesting issue. You may have thought I just threw in that seemingly offhand morsel about Parkinson's earlier, you know, being age appropriate? But I'm not that careless a writer. Why, just this morning — in the *New York Times*? — an article reported how Pope John Paul II blasted affluent societies because of their "fetish for staying-young-forever medical cures." The Pope, we are told, is to be admired as a model for "the inevitability of old age and illness." The Vatican psychiatrist (wouldn't God serve that function? I asked myself) remarked that it's "precisely in the disease — pain, old age, dying and death —that one can perceive the truth of life in a clearer way." Sure, sure, I thought. Tell that to that nice young actor who at thirty-five had to give up his career. Parkinson's. Imagine, a spastic actor!

But wait, maybe the pontiff is on to something. Maybe this fiendish fervour for youth forever is a kind of madness. My therapist's ingenuous question about life's relativity — what is "age appropriate?" — it appears now, was prescient, predicting that day when those who choose to grow old gracefully will be social outcasts. When it will no longer be appropriate to be age appropriate, if you follow my logic.

Undeterred, you tooted the same tune, warning, "You will be surrounded by women who will want to know why you haven't availed yourself of the opportunity to look your best. They'll take your contrariness as a personal affront, rather like a hostess might feel when, arriving at her home as a dinner guest, you appeared in old grubbies. You hadn't bothered to change, you see."

You gazed at me long and hard, comfortable in your skin. Your creping skin, baldpate, doughnut middle. Your milky eyes with the fat pouches beneath. You looked kindly upon me.

In order for you to truly appreciate the effort it took for me to say what I said at this point in our discussion, which I will soon recount, you must first understand what I was internalizing. The computer image, the "before" me — that is, the present me — still fresh, my self-image was, well, fragile. But perhaps I shouldn't berate myself so. I seem to have a lot of company. Did you know a recent issue of *Psychology Today* reported that sixty million North Americans don't like their nose? Thirty million don't like their chin? Six million their eyes?

After chatting with you, however, Doctor Tucker, it appears there's more to me that deserves displeasure than I was formerly aware of. You see, I don't know what I really look like. For instance, times when, checking myself in the mirror of the ladies' room in a splendid theatre, say, the Pantages or Princess of Wales, my face looks radiant beneath an incandescent gouache of rainbow rouge, my skin, alive and smooth as if air-brushed. I congratulate myself on having escaped the ravages of ageing. The same holds true when examining photographs taken from a flattering angle, the camera lens blurring nasty details. Yet, other times, when stealing a quick glance into a car window on a dull day, I'm startled by the stark reflection of a stranger. Who is she and when did she get here? Is this me? I ask myself. Which one of the many *me's* is real? What *is* reality, Doctor?

The fact is, having no stable perception of what I look like and by extension who the real me is, I was on tenuous emotional ground when challenged by you. Nevertheless, I could feel a growing rebelliousness. What had begun as doubt, the unease of a supplicant, turned to annoyance and was at this point a simmering anger.

"Yes, rejecting the opportunity modern science has offered, you'll have offended those around you," you persisted, no doubt discomfited by my long silence. "Friends will wonder if you were too stingy to spend the money. Too selfish to please your husband. Confronted with the weight of social disapproval how will you feel then?"

"*You* don't seem to have felt the need, Doctor."

"That's a whole other issue," you harrumphed.

"You mean you don't want to go there?" I asked, delighting in the colloquialism.

The room must have suddenly become hot, because your cheeks reddened and you loosened your shirt collar, shifting slightly in your seat.

"This is not about me," you protested.

"It isn't?" I asked, genuinely surprised.

"Clearly, Ms. Enfeld, you have a problem. Now, if there's nothing else...?"

This last exchange came across rather testily I thought. No matter, for some reason you evidently had had enough of me and abruptly stood, signally our interview was over. Then, recovering, you offered up a pleasant smile. "Well, now, I see you need some time to consider. Take my card. Think it over and when you decide give my receptionist a ring."

I got up from my seat and put on my coat. We gave one another a last hard assessment. My scrutiny began at the top: lonely exposed scalp, greyish beard, the pelican sac just below it; lingered on your abdominous paunch then scooted back up to meet your gaze. I took your proffered calling card, shook your hand, threw you my most glittering smile, and left.

On the way home, I reflected. My mother at seventy sprang into my mind's eye. I remembered her at my home for a dinner party, how lovely she looked, with her ibis white hair, lucent skin gently lined, its flush the afterglow at sunset; her opal eyes. She'd grown fleshy over the years, true, giving her short figure the look of a dumpling. Still, one could see she'd been a beauty. That evening she drew me to one side and whispered, "Those two boys" (forty-something *boys*?), "the heavy one there in the corner, and the one beside him, could stand a little *shmaltz* (chicken fat) on his bones...?" nodding in their direction. "Do you believe, they were coming on to me!"

I admit to being taken aback by her words, though I had earlier noted her sitting between the two men on the settee, the singular attention they seemed to be settling on her; the unmistakable looks of, well, admiration. She was beaming and I could tell she did believe their deference to be flirtatious. And why not? She felt pretty, and *young*. Were they just being attentive to an old woman or was she right?

My therapist merely shrugged when I told him about the incident. That's when he asked, *"Do you think it age appropriate?"*

Envision, Doctor Tucker, were she to submit to your examination: the computer will show her "before" in black and white, creping and sagging, puffing and flabbing. And "after," full colour, lineless as moulded plastic; neck smooth and upright, a pillar; tummy tucked, thighs and eyes lipo-sucked. She'll look not seventy, but, say, fifty ... *forty*...?

Never before had I understood, as I do now, Picasso's women, their fractured faces, angular cubist planes, how they jolt us from our comfortable perceptions to seeing from a startling new perspective. I ask you, doctor, (as I will ask my therapist): with her newly-purchased face and figure, photoshopped of

any signs of having lived, would the advances — perceived or actual — of those two young men now be age appropriate? I leave you with that last thought. I've decided to take a pass. Yours truly,
Rose Enfield

Shyandeleh's Real Estate

THE DUBIN HOUSE LIBRARY TV IS ON, just loud enough: McCain ... *error to withdraw* ... *Iraq* ... Yeah, more kids goin' off to die. Pops used to say he'd cut his kids' hands off before letting any son of his become fodder for some politician's mistakes. But Jeanne doesn't want to hear none a that, she's got enough troubles of her own.

Jeanne is peering into the library's large fish tank as she's done every day since moving into Dubin Geriatric, gazing at the silver-white she calls Queenie. Queenie's her favourite. Puffy strawberry-red crown and shimmering metallic scales; plump as a plum. Perhaps *that's* the bond they have in common, but Jeanne's not happy about the plump part, doesn't like looking like a plum. She watches Queenie as she re-establishes her claim to her property, flitting in and around the sandcastle, circling its portals and turrets, gliding along the parapet, then floats to the edge of the glass, stops, and with great dark eyes stares out at Jeanne as if to challenge her, reminding her once again that she's the intruder. Outside looking in. Jeanne doesn't need reminding. Then the fish — re-evaluating Jeanne thinks — purses its astonishing red lips and blows a bubble-kiss. Queenie must know how regal she looks (for a fish): she spreads her split tail, fanning it out on either side, a veil of gossamer; seconds later she sharply flicks it — a gesture Jeanne takes as an acknowledgment — and floats back to the castle to take up her guard.

Reaching over to the walker beside her armchair, Jeanne lifts her toiletry bag from the handlebar and rests it in her lap. A tremour unsteadies her fingers as she unzips the bag, withdraws her silver compact, opens it and examines herself in its mirror, turning her face side-to-side, critical of what she sees. Her skin lacks that natural blush it used to have, probably because she's shut up inside all the time now. Light hairs poke out under her chin — stubborn hairs tremouring hands can no longer tweeze. She frets about her weight (she's always fretting about her weight) — too many pounds, too much pastry. The food's so lousy here she has to fill herself up with pies and ice cream. Once was, she was tiny and petite, Shayndeleh, the pretty one. Now, now she's a lump — that's what she calls herself — and that makes her miserable. Queenie's swimming about in the water. Sure, plump as a plum is pleasing, *on a fish*. Jeanne's eyes stare back at her through the compact mirror; glacier-green and normally clear, today they're clouded and cheerless. Replacing the compact, she takes a Kleenex from the bag and wipes sniffles from her nostrils, thinking of yesterday when she and her niece Tzipporah stood gazing into this very same fish tank — well, Jeanne thinks it was yesterday; days, weeks, months, years, slip one into the other. Yesterday then, that's when she put it to her niece: the next time you come to visit, I won't be here, I'll be gone, on a bus to *somewhere*.

Of course Tzippie might not come to see her again; it wouldn't surprise Jeanne. Her niece never comes to see her anyway. She *says* she visits every week, but she doesn't. Jeanne would know, wouldn't she? Well, anyway, Jeanne *knows* Tzippie hasn't been here for at least six months, except of course for yesterday (she *thinks* it was yesterday), when Jeanne said she was planning to take herself away on a bus.

She told her niece something else yesterday, too, something Tzippie didn't like. Sure, she *wouldn't*, seeing herself as a good person. You'd think she was one a those Christian ladies carrying casseroles to the sick, or ladling in soup kitchens on

Sundays! Well, too bad if Tzippie didn't like what she had to say. She was mad? She'll get glad. As for Jeanne, she'd felt wretched and wistful, that was sure; but more than that, angry, and blurted out: Sure, nobody pushed *them* outa *their* home. Tzippie didn't know how to answer *that* one.

Jeanne spreads open the toiletry bag and with trembling fingers riffles through its contents, something she does every day: a lipstick, compact, hairbrush, papers with scribbling, old cheques, yellowed snapshots of her daughter Rachel and son Arnie when they were little, her address book with names of all the people who have disappeared. That's what people do when they're old, they disappear.

Now Jeanne, Shayndeleh, carries her whole life around in this little plastic toiletry bag and lives with strangers. They don't even know from *gefilte* fish, or *borscht* or brisket. Would you want to be thrown in with a bunch of greyheads just because you're all old? she puts to anyone who will listen. Now she lives in one room, with one cupboard, a three-drawer chest and an old battle-axe Jeanne calls a bitch. Tzippie says Shayndeleh — actually, she called her Jennie, which she hates — used to reside across the way, in the apartment building with the turquoise balconies, and points out the unit where Jeanne and Maury made their home when he was alive, when the whole family, her brothers and sisters, all nine, their spouses and kids and their kids' kids, used to crowd in and talk and argue and laugh together, even cry. Before then, she and Maury lived in a row home on Raritan. Jeanne remembers those times because she recalls the day Arnie drove through her old neighbourhood on the way to bringing her here, to Dubin House. How could she forget *that* day?

*

Shayndeleh's crying, protesting, morose and scared because of where Arnie's taking her. He's saying it's simply a trial. See how she gets along; after all, he only checked her out of

Cooper General just a half hour ago and she's been there a whole month. Her neighbour, Mr. Tannenbaum, told the family he'd find her Thursday mornings in the building laundry room crying and pounding the dryer. Tzippie said Jeanne was screamin' and cussin' like a pornographic parrot. And Rachel and Arnie, *they* claim Charles the Super found her kicking her car an' wailin'. Well, he's a liar! She *never*! Even if it *was* true, wouldn't *they* kick *their* tires if they came out into freezing cold to find a flat! Now Arnie's sayin' Dubin House is just a trial, wait and see what Dr. Rothman says. What does he *think* he's gonna say? That's like Arnie; never hears what *I* want; just rides right over like it counts for nothin'. Wait till his feet are in *my* moccasins!

Arnie lives in Chicago; it's the place where architects are born he says. He must of forgot he was born right *here*, in New Jersey, Jeanne thinks; that his *father* — who was only a mechanic after all and drove cab weekends to make an extra buck — sent him through school.

Arnie's wife Laura is *goyishe*. In Jeanne's opinion, Laura and Arnie — the two of 'em — are *under*-Jewish, bad as *over*-Jewish like Tzippie. Once in a Purim, Laura will come with him for a visit — *if* he comes at all, which Jeanne is not admitting. *If* he does, he "stops in" on his way to somewhere else. Now, she guesses, he's here to make sure she actually moves into Dubin Geriatric — so she, Shayndeleh, isn't "a worry" to anybody.

Jeanne stops crying and clamps her lips together, observing him. He's still got a healthy head of hair, though greying, but she notices he's getting thick around the waist; the slope of his shoulders has grown more pronounced and deeply etched creases web out from the corners of his eyes — *her* eyes, his best feature. Her son is beginning to show his fifty-five years and he's taken to complaining about his grown daughters, too busy with their own lives to think of him or their mother. *That's* a good one. Yeah, he's a funny duck. A good man, but stubborn, got his own ideas. Well, *she* needs some attention paid.

She wants to drive through her old neighbourhood on the way to see what's become of the area and the house on Raritan before she never sees them again. Everyone says a drive-through's too dangerous — drugs and guns and gangs. Nothin' left of the Towers and Stanley movie houses, the shops, the big Department Stores — Gimbels and Sears and Lits. Boarded-up, burnt down. That's what the sixties did. Evangelical churches an' liquor stores now. But the car doors are locked and she's with Arnie and it's daytime. Besides, they're just driving down her old street.

Halloween skeletons and sheeted ghosts swing and twist, eerie in the slanted light of October's late-afternoon sun; jack-o-lanterns perch on stoops, in windows, grin, mocking, as if it is all a joke. Yeah, and the joke's on me, she thinks.

The red-bricked row homes have darkened over the years; lining the sidewalks, leafy oaks canopy the street, and fences — chain link, white picket, wrought iron — cosset yards of uncut grasses, all together giving the block a shadowy, cloistered character.

Arnie slows the car and draws down the window. "There's your house, Shayndeleh, 513. It's looking good." He stops the car.

"Yeah. Needs paint."

"Mm. Shutters weathered. Pediments all settled," he says, sweeping his glance over the doors along the row. Arnie, the architect, notices these things. "Street's recovered some. No boarded-up windows, anyway. New storm door," he observes of 513.

Jeanne peers up and down the street, remembering how in summers Arnie and Rachel and the kids on the block played hopscotch on the sidewalk and jacks on the stoop. How Maury stood in the doorway, screaming, "Quit runnin' on the grass!" and Jeanne would shout, "Get away from the door and quit yellin'! Do you want the neighbours to think you're from South Philly?" Of course, he *was* from South Philly, she smiles inwardly, back when it was all immigrant Jewish, before the Jews moved out and the blacks moved in. Now South Philly has moved *here*, to South Jersey, to the neighbourhood, to Raritan. All black. Used to be there was a Giordano down the block and a Giardelli a couple a houses down, a Patterson next door and a Katinsky across the way.

It was a quiet place then. The grownups mostly inside or maybe out, sitting on lawn chairs or gliders on their patch of patio in July and August, gazing at lightning bugs flitting about the lawn. The younger kids'd chase after the little blinking fireflies an' catch 'em in their cupped hands then let them fly off again. Arnie and Rachel — teenagers by that time — hung out on the corner with friends, sneakin' a cigarette under the beam of the lamplight. Now, driving down the street with Arnie, all up and down Raritan everyone's out barbecuing, making a lot of noise, the teenagers lollin' on the stoop, the little kids chasin' around the yard. They must all know everyone on the block, Jeanne thinks, but they seem closed off from one another, neighbour from neighbour; walled off, or *in*, as if the fences assured them of privacy. There *wasn't* no fences squarin' off the lawns when Jeanne and the Giordanos and Pattersons and Katinskys lived in these houses.

Arnie shifts his foot from the brake to the accelerator and continues slowly down the street. Jeanne watches out the open window, keeping her eyes on her house for as long as she can, then fixes her gaze ahead, on the cars parked on either side. She and Maury used to own a Chevy, and across from them Millie had two cars parked in front, *two!* Arnie eases his car between the rows. Jeanne can't help but notice the cars are newish, probably middle-priced, and in fairly good condition. This surprises her.

Yeah, neighbourhood's all black now — *shvartze*. Everyone used to call 'em coloureds back then. Arnie says she can't use "coloureds" anymore — not *shvartze* either. That's ridiculous. Her family — all ten kids — used to live in a poor neighbourhood, above her father Louis's dry goods store — his *shmatteh* business, on 11th Street, just off the Delaware River Bridge. All black. We pulled ourselves up and outa there. Funny how things come 'round.

They had a Holy Roller church on the corner. She laughs to herself, remembering. Well, we called it that. Probably was Baptist, she realizes now. She and her brothers and sisters used to climb up onto a box and peek in an' see all of 'em rocking an' rolling, clapping and swaying, and in summer when the windows were open they could hear them singin' and shoutin' *Oh, Lord, Oh, Lord!*

She examines the cars parked along the curb, remarking once again on their decent condition. Nobody owned a car in those long-ago days, unless you were rich and had a model-T. Everyone called it a Tin Lizzie. Pops had a horse and buggy and kept the horse in a stable at the end of the street. That was then. It's all different now. He sold the store, the kids grew up, Jeanne married Maury, and the two moved to 513 Raritan.

Everything was good until the riots happened down South and President Kennedy sent in troops. Used to be everybody got along, even in the neighbourhood with the Holy Rollers — they knew their place and everything was fine. (Arnie says she can't say *they knew their place* either, but why not?) Till some nut killed the President and the black preacher who climbed to the top of a mountain, like Moses, and had a dream. Then people went crazy.

Yeah, the real estate guys know how to make a buck. Broke the block — that's what they used to call it — an' the Pattersons an' Giordanos an' Katinskys got out quick. For a while, she and Maury hung in; *these* ones had jobs and dressed their kids nice. Spoke real polite. Then, they, *gonifs*, started movin' in riff-raff and their black brothers panicked too and followed the Patterson an' Giordanos an' Katinskys. She and Maury were the only whites left on the block. Well, I'm right back where I started, Jeanne remembers thinking (bitterly). Things turned so bad she and Maury got what they could for the house and fled.

Street's come back up, though — at least somewhat; Arnie was right, she acknowledges, gazing out the side window again. She never woulda believed it. Government project: you promise to fix up a house, it's yours for a dollar! Course, who'd want to live there? The street's still ruined. Katinsky's place boarded up; Giordano's, windows smashed through, gaping blind eyes ... same, same on down the row.

She scrutinizes the houses, trying to recall who lived in each before everything changed. Well, the homes're in better shape than she expected. But before cruising the street Arnie drove her around to the back alley, an unwashed neck on a (partial-ly) scrubbed face: boarded up windows; weed lot; overturned garbage pails, their refuse spilling onto asphalt drives; garages begging for a fresh coat of paint.

Still, she observes as Arnie continues cautiously down the front of the street, still, the children for the most part are dressed clean and neat in runners, jeans, and sweats cut off and ragged at the shoulders — what kids wear these days; here and there, homes have lace curtains, nice lawn chairs and tidy beds with the last of the fall flowers. It's true the bricks have darkened with age, but some have been newly pointed.

Arnie's car slows almost to a stop as he approaches the corner. "Oh," Jeanne's heart skips a beat. She's caught the eye of a very large black man seated in a lawn chair in his yard, just inside the gate; no car parked at the curb to block Jeanne's view. She can see him quite clearly. He's black as Africa. His eyeballs are very white and he's wearing a white T-shirt, black trousers and baseball cap, a beer bottle in his hand. She takes in his thick upper arms, construction-worker hands, splayed trunk-like thighs. For an instant his eyes lock with hers. The suspicion she sees there knocks her back and a surly defensiveness to his mien sends shivers down her spine. He sits forward as if on alert. Even so, his body has a settled-in look — the way it occupies the entire chair, proprietary. *Whadjou doin' in my neighbourhood, whitey?* Jeanne hears these words as clearly as if they were said aloud. In fact, she could swear he shouted them. Gripping the door handle, she thrusts her face toward the man. Some crazy lady in the car is screaming, *No! This is my street! My neighbourhood. My house up the block!* Arnie drives on without a backward glance. He hasn't heard a thing.

*

Even now, eyeing the fish tank in Dubin House, watching Queenie stake out her home, her castle, Shayndeleh relives the grief she'd felt, the overwhelming sense of loss on leaving so much behind, triggered by seeing the house on Raritan again. Maury said she'd not be able to fit the dining table and china closet or their bedroom chest into the new apartment with the turquoise balconies. Nor could she bring the patio glider; and she'd have to do their laundry in a common room on the ground floor. There'd be no kids playing on the stoop or chasing fireflies on the lawn. Course that was a long *long* time ago, she admits, though time blurs.

Rachel, Arnie, and Tzippie all say Jeanne moved into Dubin Geriatric three years ago, but she doesn't know what three years means. Three years, three months, three days. There's only the distant past, no *now* now. Only a field of greyheads — that's what she calls them — women mostly, asleep in wheelchairs, their chins dropped to their chests, their shoulders sagging, listless. Some — those who remember where they are, or *who* they are — play Bingo. Every day. Every evening. *What's new?* Tzippie asks her. Is Tzippie *stupid?*

Jeanne doesn't play Bingo, or even gin rummy anymore; only follows Tzippie's finger pointing across the way to her apartment building with the turquoise balconies. She has no sense of connection to it, her former life but a short walk across a driveway, narrow expanse of green and a parking lot. Still, on good days she relives those times as if they were today. Oh, her place — *wherever* that was — was the size of a card table, but it had a *proper living room and dining area and a separate bedroom* and enough space to cram her sprawling, scrapping, chaotic family into. They — the grownups and all the children — gathered there for Chanukah, and after funerals everyone crowded in for *shiva* and laughed and mourned and told stories, remembering. And ate. They're Jewish, they eat.

When she moved out she left her Lladro figurines behind, her Bird of Happiness woodcarving, Victorian tier table, sofa and oversized Sony TV. Now everything's shrunk to one room, a bed, an armoire and a three-drawer chest. And a nutcase for a roommate. All the rest of her belongings, but for the clothes, fit into a solitary plastic toiletry purse. Friends, neighbours, community — Solly the butcher, Fagie the deli owner, Doris, her hairdresser — mere reflections in a dog-eared address book.

Queenie peers out at Jeanne through the glass and makes puck-puck movements with her lips. Orange and calico goldfish hover above emerald and lapis lazuli; gauzy tails, fine as filigree, fan the water; leafy plants shiver with each ripple and from a filter bubbles burble and rise like carbonated fizz. Jeanne catches the fluorescent-white flicker of the library TV screen out of the corner of her eye and an announcer is saying something she can't make out; shouts and chanting fill the background with white noise. She turns from the fish tank to look.

A black man has been elected president. A black family is moving into the White House — the white house! *So, is it good for the Jews?* Jeanne wonders and smiles a little crooked smile, aware she's being funny. Someone turns up the volume and she hears the announcer's excited voice: "Barack..." and "Michelle..." and, "the next first lady of the United States!" Michelle is wearing a black dress, its front an explosion of red. The children are between them and they're all holding hands, smiling and waving. He's tall, trim and handsome, flawless in a crease-free black suit and starched whiter-than-white dress shirt. Jeanne has a hawk eye for these things. She could do without Michelle's dress, but still, the new first lady makes an impression.

Jeanne doesn't know quite what to make of it all. She long ago left the Lordy-Lordy Holy Rollers behind, but now a *black* man *from Harvard* is moving into the nation's *White* House. Course she has worked with some lovely black women — well, not really black; more coffee brown — very thoughtful and polite, when she worked at City Federal after Maury got sick, but then there was that menacing beer-swilling man black as Africa who'd taken over her Raritan home. Driving through her old neighbourhood, seeing him, gave her a jolt. She was angry, not so much, she has determined, at the man as at Arnie, who'd given notice on her apartment and was *putting her in a Home.* Humph! *Home.* That's one a them words that pretend to mean one thing and really mean another. Who did they think they were kidding? Did Arnie think she wouldn't notice? Did he think she wouldn't catch on to what he and Rachel and Tzippie and all the rest a them, *including* Dr. Rothman, were plotting? She wasn't *that* addled.

Time, the years, blur — a lifetime of memories. No new excitements, the very *stuff* of memories, to define the days. Maybe that's why the old, like Jeanne herself — *"seniors,"* another one a them words — can't remember an hour past, only decades.

Jeanne gazes at Queenie, her fanciful pompom, her big dark fish-eyes gazing back. Maybe Jeanne's imagining it, but she swears Queenie winked (do fish have lashes?). Jeanne, Shayndeleh, will come every morning, afternoon and evening to visit with her silent friend who every day travels nowhere as if going *somewhere.* She'll watch in admiration as Queenie claims her castle, protects it, intuitively understanding its importance to her own existence.

If she hasn't already left on a bus to somewhere, well then next time Tzippie — or Arnie or Rachel (although they *never* come, *none* of 'em) — comes to visit, Jeanne will be here in the library, her eyes drinking in the calico and gold, orange, blue and black, as they streak to the surface and hang vertically suspended, gulping in air and flecks of food. Queenie will break away and dart back to her castle to re-establish ownership. Every so often she'll float over to the glass and blink at Jeanne, spread her tail and blow kisses.

"See," Jeanne will point out to Tzippie, "See how the silver and white one with the pompadour stays near to home? How she guards it? See how she *recognizes* me?"

And Tzippie will answer, "Oh, Jenny, it's a fish!"

Shayndeleh will set her lips in a straight line and say not a word.

Acknowledgements

The stories appearing in *Aspects of Nature* could not have reached maturity without the significant guidance and support of teachers and mentors Janette Turner Hospital, Helen Weinzweig and Matthew Corrigan. Matthew Corrigan, professor at York University and my first creative writing teacher, has remained a source of constant support, offering me the benefit of his time and editing skills, his wide and deep understanding of literature and writing, a source of my continued learning and growth over the years.

My thanks to Rick Archbold, author and award-winning editor, who helped me to reveal the one story in the three competing for dominance, culminating in the romantic comedy *Moon over Mandalay*. To author and long-time friend Julie Brickman, for her on-going support, encouragement and belief in the worthiness of my writing. To friends Brenda Silver and Rheba Adolph for their valued feedback on an early draft of a most challenging story. And to my brother-in-law, Paul Friedman, for his web design and editing, for which he is paid only with my gratitude.

To Inanna editor-in-chief, Luciana Ricciutelli, I owe my gratitude for having heard, and given recognition to, my "voice." She has allowed for the kind of fulfilment that happens only when one's creative life comes together in a way that makes sense of all that went before. And to Renée Knapp for her marketing guidance and efforts, giving a public face to *Aspects of Nature*, and for the work and time involved in editing and posting of my numerous blogs.

I am so lucky to have had the support, feedback and camaraderie of friends, and of my writing colleagues: the Sterling Farm group, who came together in an intensive workshop at Queens with Janette Turner Hospital and stayed in touch over some thirty years: Nancy Carroll, Barb Fraser (now deceased), Barb Feldman, Gregg Blake and Anna Jaimet (now Deirdre Hart); the Lobsters writers' group (co-founders Elaine Batcher, K.D. Miller, Kim Aubrey) in Toronto, which grew into Red Claw Press.

Finally, to my husband, Joseph (Joe) for graciously reading many many drafts of stories, which seemed never to be "final"; and for countless times he took over the making of dinner, clean-up or shopping, so that I could go off and "get some writing done." He has always been there for me. My love to Joe and all my family for just being.

The following stories were previously published in literary journals:

"Dear Doctor" in *Fireweed* (1993);
"You Make Your Decision" in *Dandelion* (1994);
"Out to Lunch with the Girls" in *Parchment* (1994);
"Aspects of Nature" in *The Louisville Review* (2007);
"The Day of the Gorgon" in *Jewish Currents* (1999);
"Shayndeleh" in *Parchment* (as "Inside the inside Looking Outside") (2009);
"The Wind at Her Back" in *Sistersong* (1997);
"What's Going on Here, Anyway?" in *The Fiddlehead* (1996).

My thanks to all of the above journals, which considered my work worthy of publication.

Photo: Ian Willms

Rhoda Rabinowitz Green is the author of two novels, *Slowly I Turn* and *Moon Over Mandalay.* Her short fiction has been published in magazines and journals across North America, including *The Fiddlehead, The Louisville Review, Dandelion, Fireweed, Parchment, Sistersong,* and *Jewish Currents.* Her work has been nominated for a Pushcart prize and was a finalist in the Canadian Writers Union Short Prose Competition. She lives in Toronto.